CW00557195

RO

Other Series by H.P. Mallory

Paranormal Women's Fiction Series:
Haven Hollow
Midlife Spirits
Midlife Mermaid

Paranormal Shifter Series:
Arctic Wolves

Paranormal Romance Series:
Underworld
Lily Harper
Dulcie O'Neil
Lucy Westenra

Paranormal Adventure Series:
Dungeon Raider
Chasing Demons

Detective SciFi Romance Series:
The Alaskan Detective

Academy Romance Series:
Ever Dark Academy

Reverse Harem Series:
Happily Never After
My Five Kings

ROSE

Book 4 of The Happily Never After Series

By

HP Mallory

Copyright ©2020 by HP Mallory

License Notes

This ebook is licensed for your personal enjoyment only. This ebook may not be re-sold or given away to other people. If you would like to share this book with another person, please purchase an additional copy for each recipient. If you're reading this book and did not purchase it, or it was not purchased for your enjoyment only, then please return to Smashwords.com or your favorite retailer and purchase your own copy. Thank you for respecting the hard work of this author.

10 Chosen Ones:

When a pall is cast upon the land,
Despair not, mortals,
For come forth heroes ten.
One in oceans deep,
One the flame shall keep,
One a fae,
One a cheat,
One shall poison grow,
One for death,
One for chaos,
One for control,
One shall pay a magic toll.

Rose Red:

Nightshade,
Hemlock,
Aconite,
the Queen of Poisons she shall be,
and leach the life from a goddess,
who taints the world tree.

ONE
CARMINE

The hinges of the iron door squeak, even as I try desperately for stealth.

The lag between the changing of the guard is pitifully short. I don't have the time I need to speak to him properly, but I don't see many options. My Uncle Spyros is planning something large and extravagant for arriving dignitaries. If I'm to talk to him, it has to be now.

I take a cautious step inside the cell, and backpedal just as quickly, tripping on the long hem of my dress. The intense odor emanating from inside the cell is like having something sharp jabbed into my nose. I've always been sensitive to smells. Something to do with my mother's heritage, or so Uncle tells me.

"Princess?" my maid, Elsie, inquires from further up the corridor. She has a white-knuckled grip on the stair rail, and her eyes make the circuit from my position before the cell and the stairwell behind her every few seconds or so.

The sight of her perched there, steels my nerves. My poor Elsie has risked so much for this clandestine meeting already. While I'd done the

1

fairly simple job of pilfering the wine from supper one night, my lady's maid had been the one to go downstairs and ply the guards with spirits. The one who'd tolerated the pawing hands of drunken soldiers in order to steal and then copy the key to Draven's cell.

Taking a drag of the stale air from the hall, I step inside the cell once more and wade into the murky interior. Straw and seed scrape beneath the low heels that Uncle insisted I wear beneath the ensemble. The ridiculously thick red dress is going to be stained with something by the end of the night, so it might as well be whatever foulness has clogged Draven's cell.

The birdseed is a problem, though. It rolls beneath my heels and makes even the simplest step treacherous. The guards think it's funny to pelt Draven with it, even though most of them know better. For the sake of the Gods, they shared the same barracks, ate at the same table in the great hall. I know at least one of them was being trained specifically by Draven for the honor of guarding me when Draven was away.

How things have changed...

After the attack in the Lordell Mountains, in a valley so remote and uninteresting that most of our maps had no record of it, now the place is unlikely to ever be forgotten.

It was the location where my mother and a small army of men met their ends. Draven was the only one to stagger back to Ascor, charred almost beyond recognition, but still alive after surviving a dragon attack. He should have been praised as a hero for returning and delivering the account of the attack to us.

Instead, Uncle clapped him in irons and threw him into the dungeons to die. And there Draven has remained. The guards cast lots on whether starvation, infection, or thirst will take him first.

I begged to know the reason why Draven had been treated so poorly day and night for a week, until Uncle forbade any further talk on the matter, punctuating the order with a sharp slap.

I haven't had the courage to ask again, sure I'll receive more than a sting in my cheek next time. I feel remarkably fragile without my steadfast huntsman at my back.

I find Draven splayed in the furthest corner from the stairwell, where the light rarely hits and enough water runs down the stone after the rains to soothe his burns. He's fortunate it's been a rainy summer in Ascor—he has a shallow pool to lay in often enough.

My steps falter a few feet shy of Draven's only visible limb. A foot, bare and blessedly free of blisters. Shifter healing can be remarkable, but Draven's has been stymied somehow. Something my father did or the result of dragon fire? I can't say.

"Draven," I venture cautiously, speaking as loud as I dare, with the guard rotation so close at hand. "Draven, can you hear me?"

A soft moan in response and then his foot twitches, withdraws back into shadow and I hear the clink of the chain sliding against itself as he moves. He's not imprisoned in a cell, but he's fastened to the floor, probably unable to so much as stand.

My heart thumps harder as a shape begins to shuffle half into sight. Draven has never actually moved toward me, too injured or incapacitated by fever to respond to my attempts to speak to him.

And this time is no different, it seems.

The shape that slides from the darkness and peers up at me isn't Draven. It's not even male. It's one of the prisoners of war that Spyros has been holding for trial. She's pretty, I have to admit, even after spending Gods knows how long in this dungeon with little to no washing. She appears to be a woman in her prime, with milky skin whose beauty isn't dulled by the thin layer of grime. Lips as pink as cherry blossoms, color high in her cheeks—a flush of red, like a rose.

In fact, the more I look at her, the more she appears like a floral mural. Eyes like purple dahlia, a shade that escapes being black by the presence of light. Skin lily-white. Hair as pale and muted as silver ragwort.

I dislike her at once, though the reasons for my animosity are ridiculous. But she's beautiful, even unwashed and a little feral-looking. She reminds me of Neva, who was beautiful even as a girl when I was (and am) so woefully plain, just like mother. The reminder of Neva is a jab of pain just under my ribs. I've missed the anniversary of Neva's passing. Again.

But the true reason heat flushes into my cheeks and shame wriggles in my belly is petty.

She's here with him when I can't be.

"Who are you?" I ask a little tartly.

"An excellent question," the woman mutters, more to herself than me. "I wish I knew."

"What do you mean?"

She sighs. "Last I can recall is Elysium fields, a dark sea, and swimming, screaming bears."

I blink down at her in shock, most of my enmity evaporating when I realize this poor, condemned woman is quite mad. She scrambles for the other corner when I continue to stare.

"Ignore the rambling," Draven croaks from the gloom. "I think she's a Wonderland native. She's not going to make any sense."

My heart strains the prison of my ribs in an attempt to get to him. He's speaking. Finally! I've missed hearing his voice.

But the same time, this *isn't* his voice. Draven's voice used to be a pleasant baritone, a rich, melodic thing that never failed to sing me to sleep on lonely nights. I'd so often been a naughty girl, calling him into my room not to put me to sleep, as I claimed. I'd spent those evenings peering at him through my lashes, watching his mouth move and letting his voice caress me. Because it was the only part of him to ever touch any part of me, no matter how ardently I wished otherwise.

Now his beautiful voice is gone. He's hoarse, deep, and scratchy, like the voice of the raven form he can assume.

Back to the woman… If she's from Wonderland, Draven is quite right. She won't make any sense as all the Wonderland inhabitants are insane. "What is her name?" I ask.

"She calls herself Ia when she's lucid."

I nod but I can't say I care much to discuss the mad woman any longer. Instead, I want to figure out how to free Draven, how to help him escape this awful place. I sink down onto my haunches, extending an imploring hand toward him. "Draven… how… how can I free you?"

"You can't," he scoffs.

"There must be a way! I'll free you… I can get the key to your chains…"

"And then what?"

I swallow hard because I haven't thought that far ahead. "I'll... I'll take you away from here. Far, far away. We can..."

He laughs, though it sounds more like a cough with his new, gravelly tone.

"Go where? I'm little better than Ia. Lucidity comes and goes and I... I'm not well. I can't protect you. And I won't have you venturing into danger for me."

Giving up the pretense of politeness, I drop my gloved hand back down to my side and shuffle into the dark and smelly corner. I have an inkling what my uncle has brought the dignitaries here to discuss. I can't face the prospect of a loveless marriage until I've seen Draven one last time. Until I've kissed him. Until I've loved him.

The last, errant thought causes blood to rush into my cheeks. I'm truly a wicked girl, to think such things. He's injured. And even if he weren't, he will never care for me as I care for him. He's been my protector since I can remember. He'll never think of me as anything more than Leon's child, the poor, orphaned princess. To ask anything more of him is wrong.

I stagger a step when I encounter something warm and solid in the darkness. I lose my footing and sprawl on top of the shape, skirts flying wide like a scarlet fan. My legs tangle with the shape and I realize, with a jolt and warm flush of desire,

that my legs are wound between Draven's, my
thighs straddling one of his and the knee of the
other leg rubbing deliciously against my clothes.

His hands shoot out to steady me, coming to
rest on my waist. He raises himself slightly from
the ground. His breath fans across my neck and
ruffles my hair when he speaks. Goosebumps riot
across my skin. He's so close. It would be so easy
for him to hike my skirts and take me like this. I
don't care that he's covered in filth. He's Draven,
my unrequited love and I will take whatever he
offers me.

"Are you alright, Princess?"

"I'm fine. Did I hurt you?"

"Not badly."

"I'm sorry, I should move."

I try to scramble backward. I'm still not sure
what madness possessed me to visit him tonight
without being better prepared. If I'd been thinking,
I could have stolen into the cell with shoots of my
aloe plant. I can feel the burns now, shiny and
swollen, on parts of his body. There are herbal
remedies I can concoct that could heal them in
short order.

Stupid, stupid girl not to have thought of any
of this before it was too late.

Before I can move more than an inch down his
thigh, Draven catches me. He sits up, hauling me

into his chest, lifting me slightly off him and arranges me so I'm straddling him properly.

"Don't move," he mutters into my ear. "You can't imagine how good it feels to have you with me. Stay still just a moment, love."

And though I know he doesn't mean anything by the word, my mind still spins out an elaborate, delicious lie that my handsome huntsman truly does feel the same way for me.

"I'm hurting you," I argue weakly, even as I settle my head into the hollow between his shoulder and his throat. "You're injured."

"I'll bear it," he replies shortly. "Stay."

I can't argue with that, so I curl myself as closely as I can with the ridiculous red skirts in the way. I'll definitely have to change before supper tonight. I don't mind. Not with Draven's arms wrapped around me. Even the smell of the cell is bearable now, with him holding me tight.

I gently skim my fingers over his body, assessing the injuries by feel. They mostly appear to be burns, though I'm afraid a few patches have become infected. Sores pop along the joints, where he's forced to move the injured skin. There are a few deep score marks, like he was cut with a blade or a very determined man with a whip.

Tears prick my eyes. He must be in so much pain and I can't even free him from this prison. My oldest and truest companion is rotting while I do nothing. If I'm to marry, I'll assume the throne soon with a foreign king at my side. Elsie tells me men will agree to many things while inside a woman. Perhaps I can coax my new husband into releasing Draven? Even if I can convince him exile is best, I'll have saved Draven's life. As a huntsman, he can survive anywhere and can return to the House of Corvid without incident.

"I'm going to get you out," I whisper. "I swear it to all the Gods, I'm going to get you out. I won't let them hurt you any longer."

Draven presses his face into my hair, inhaling deeply. His fingers push into the slick material of my dress, his hands as hot as brands, even through the fabric. The burns, or just my own fevered imagination?

Imagination, I decide, because I swear he turns his head just a fraction to kiss me. His lips certainly brush the hollow beneath my ear. The contact is so intimate, it sends forbidden pleasure zinging through me. I buck a little in surprise.

Then he releases me, hands falling away from my body, curling in on himself like a boy being chastised.

"I'm sorry," he croaks. "I shouldn't have put my hands on you, Princess."

No! I want to argue. No, I want his hands on me. Fingers in me. I want *him*. But I don't get a chance to say or do more because Elsie appears in the doorway of the dungeon, quivering and pale as a ghost.

"They're coming, Princess," she whispers, flicking her gaze toward the far end of the hall.

Sure enough, if I strain my ears, I can hear the thud of heavy feet and the rattle of armor as a group of them move quickly toward our position.

"Go," Draven says softly. "And don't return, Princess. Whatever punishment you suffer, isn't worth it."

Lies. A beating is the worst my Uncle is likely to subject me to, and I'll take it for Draven, gladly.

"I'm coming back for you," I promise him, though he laughs at me as though I can't keep my word. "Don't you dare die before I can spring you from this... this..." There's no delicate word for it. "This shithole. Stay alive for me, Draven."

Then I turn and pelt up the corridor as fast as my ridiculous shoes will allow.

His whispered reply is almost whipped away on the wind.

"Princess..."

TWO
CARMINE

I'm covered in filth. And dirt is the least offensive stain on the silk. Uncle will be upset to learn I've ruined it, but I'll be damned if I tell him why. I'm not eager to be struck again.

Elsie is set to guard my door while I wriggle my way into the less extravagant but still beautiful blue silk gown Uncle commissioned for my last birthday. It's almost the precise shape and color of a bluebell, flaring out dramatically around my ankles. I'm secretly glad to wear it. I prefer it to the red.

The rose water in the corner is meant to perfume my chambers, but I use the softly scented stuff to scrub my skin free of dirt. It's strange, but I can make out Draven's fingerprints on my arms and on the material of my dress. I'm almost reluctant to scrub myself, as it's the only tangible evidence he's finally touched me.

You're too sentimental, Carmine, I chastise myself with a frown. *Leave the dirt and there will be questions. Scrub up now.*

But still, I hesitate over the skin of my forearms. *Draven touched me.* I can't shake the phantom feeling of his fingers pressing into my skin. He was probably delirious with pain or fever. Perhaps he'd gone a little mad, stuffed into a dark cell with only a raving woman for company. It probably had little to do with me at all. He'd have clutched at Elsie the same way. Perhaps more ardently, as he'd have no compunctions making love to a mere maid. I've known him to do so before.

My mouth screws up in distaste and I dislike the feeling of bitter jealousy that washes over me at the thought. I'm not being fair. He's at least two or three times my age and has guarded me since before I had a name to put to these feelings—a name I quite believe to be 'love'. Regardless, he's entitled to be with others. I can't selfishly horde his affection like a lovelorn dragon.

Ha. As if there were such a thing.

The scrape of the key in the lock is the only warning I get. I hastily swipe the damp cloth across the dirt on my arms and then stuff the damp cloth beneath a pillow to hide the evidence of my illicit visit. I've just spilled the last of the dirty rose water into my chamber pot and shoved the whole thing beneath my bed when someone steps into the room.

It's not Elsie, or my uncle, as I half-expect. It's a man who I'm only vaguely familiar with. He was sent ahead of one of the visiting dignitaries as his personal valet. I've seen him lurking about several times, always perched like a miserable vulture about to swoop when I'm about. A little over average height, average in appearance and garb, he wouldn't ordinarily stand out to me. His lips are thin, his expression almost always dour.

But there's more… there's something about him. I don't like the way he looks at me. I especially don't like the way he lurks in my doorway, just staring. His eyes are a strange mahogany color that appears almost red when the light hits them correctly. The color of his eyes is the only thing about him that is mildly appealing but still, I can't derive any pleasure from his gaze.

I draw myself up to my full height, which is admittedly not impressive. Neva was always taller than me, even when we were children. Still, I'm thoroughly middling and I can look him in the eye, which I do. The scoundrel ought to know his place and drop his eyes to the floor.

"You've entered the wrong room, sir," I say patiently, giving him a chance to retreat. I don't want to cause upset with his Prince before the dinner is set to take place, but if he means me ill, I want to at least try to give him an option to retreat before he's slaughtered by my guards. "My maid ought to have told you as much, Mr. Anwn."

At least, I think that's his name. All of the valets seem to bleed together in my head. Rude of me to forget.

"Anon," he corrects me, a muscle ticking ever so slightly beside his left eye.

"Apologies," I say, though my tone makes it glaringly obvious I don't mean the words.

I don't feel too terrible about my discourtesy. He's not meant to be in a woman's chambers alone, let alone a princess'. He ought to know that. Still, he doesn't move. His hands inch toward something beneath his cloak. And then I realize something alarming: why is he wearing a cloak indoors in spring?

My fevered imagination must be acting up again, because I swear he's trying to go for a... dagger? Such a move would be insanity within the castle walls. There are at least three guards stationed in this corridor—guards who will come running if I so much as sneeze, let alone scream.

Still, I drop my hand into the hidden pocket of my gown. Draven always bribed the tailor to add hidden sections into my gowns. For storage, he said sagely to the woman when she asked. For my sewing needles and any pretty flowers I wish to press. But since I turned sixteen, there's always been a blade in the interior. A small, two-inch throwing knife that Draven taught me to wield. He'd kept me in the garden afternoon after afternoon, tossing the damned thing until I could remove an apple from a fence post at fifty paces. I admit I deliberately missed more than once, just so he'd grip my wrist to show me the proper form again.

Anon takes note of the motion and something in his posture eases and he offers me a tight smile. When his hands emerge from his cloak, I don't spy a weapon. Still, I let my fingers curl around the grip of my blade, just in case.

"Your lady's maid has suffered an ague. Prince Achmed expressed concern and wishes me to accompany you to the gardens for your afternoon outing. He does not wish you to be lonely before your meeting this evening. I am at your disposal, Princess."

I continue to stare at the plain, almost unremarkable man. There is something off about him, though I can't quite put my finger on what is troubling me. Something in his bearing, perhaps. I swear I've seen a man hold himself in almost precisely the same way before. A guard? No, too indolent for a palace guard. They're stiff, rigid. Not posh or arrogant enough to be a prince, either. What is it then?

Social niceties demand an answer, even as I try to bully my poor mind into divulging the answer. My responding smile is pretty and hollow as a painted flower pot.

"Thank you, Mr. Anon, but that won't be necessary. I can find ways to occupy my time until supper. Perhaps I can take a stroll with the Prince after the meal? My night blooming jasmine is quite lovely. I've heard Prince Achmed quite likes jasmine."

Anon continues to stare at me in mute frustration until I'm forced to abandon all subtlety. I cross over to him, keeping one hand lightly tracing the blade in my pocket while the other comes to rest lightly on the back of my chamber door.

I smile sweetly at him, though I feel anything but cheerful.

"Good day, Mr. Anon. I'll see you and your Prince at supper."

And then, with a flick of my wrist, I close the door in his face.

***

Uncle Spyros has an unctuous voice and an exterior to match it.

He favors my mother that way. Shapeless and on the shorter side, as most phobetors are. A cap of auburn hair, though his is much shorter than mom's stylish bob. His eyes are a deep blue and he's paler than almost anyone I've ever had the privilege to know. The exception, of course, being Neva, who was so ashy pale, she was mistakenly declared a stillborn the first minute after her birth. My heart clenches tightly at the memory of Neva and my chest feels clammy, though the interior of the great hall is warm.

Neva.

It was my fault.

I as good as killed my sister. And I don't have the decency to remember the day my traitorous tongue condemned her. I'm truly a wicked girl and I imagine I will burn for all eternity, owing to the mistakes I've made.

I haven't really been paying much attention to what's being said around the table, too focused on strategic avoidance of Prince Achmed's straying limbs. Throughout the first course of tomato bisque, he'd been rubbing his foot along my ankle and up the length of my calf, lifting my dress as he went. A soft smirk graced his lips while he ate duck swimming in a savory sauce, all the while replacing the foot with his hand, thankfully over the material this time.

I was finally forced to shove the offending hand away from my thigh when he tried to stray up—to play along the seam that runs between my thigh and hip. He's been scowling at me ever since.

It's not that he's truly unattractive. He has a nice, angular face and the unmistakable bearing of royalty. His skin is a lovely golden-brown color, his angular jaw shaded with attractive stubble. His hair looks soft and touchable. His shoulders are broad, his waist cut lean, and muscle shows beneath his clothing. Most women would relish the thought of bearing his attentions.

But he's not Draven. He's not even a friend like Blakely Nonpareil of Sweetland, who may be the most charming prince I've ever met. I don't know Achmed and thus far? I don't care for him.

So it catches me entirely off guard when my Uncle drops the announcement casually into the conversation. I'm sure it has been building and I've been too dreadfully dense to notice, but still...

"What?" I repeat dully, staring up the line of the table to the place where my Uncle sits at the head.

He looks wrong there. Too short and too oily to sit in the chair of the late King Leon, lion-hearted king of Ascor.

Uncle Spyros' pale face bunches like parchment. He's not easy on the eyes on a good day. Dream manipulators like night hags and their male counterparts, the phobetors, range from plain to terrifyingly grotesque. When he's angry, my uncle could scare the piss out of any common variety hero at sixty paces and send them looking for a different villain to vanquish. Preferably in a land far, far away.

I've always worried there's some of that in me, as well. I share blood with him, after all. I'm not beautiful, like Neva, but I have never been called

ugly. Perhaps I've been fortunate and I'm just...
human.

"Have you been listening, girl?" You know
how I dislike repeating myself."

I flick a gaze to Anon's position, behind
Achmed, and I seize upon a ready excuse. "My
maid, Elise, has been struck with an ague, Uncle.
I'm afraid I may suffer the same fate in short order.
I feel a bit faint."

I tuck my chin and stare at my hands, affecting
a slight tremor, trying to look like the most
miserable wretch alive. It's not difficult to fake.
This whole affair is making me queasy and has
been.

Uncle's expression doesn't soften.
"Regardless, you will marry Prince Achmed within
the week and return with him to his kingdom."

I jerk my eyes up from my cuticles and stare at
him in unflattering shock. I really *should* have paid
attention while the arrangements were being
discussed so I could object. Object and do so
persistently. What in the name of Avernus is my
uncle thinking? I knew this dinner would likely end
in a marriage announcement but I did not expect…
this!

"Uncle I can't!" I splutter, shaking my head
with vehemence. "You can't send me away from
Ascor! Marry me to a worthy suitor if you like, but
I have to stay here. This… this is my home and

these are my people! My responsibility. You can't just…"

But I'm not given a chance to continue my sentence, because a bolt of pure agony strikes me between the eyes and it's all I can do not to scream. The images are not half so potent as they might be, were I asleep. They're still frightening enough to have me gnawing at the inside of my cheek to contain a whimper.

Mummy clutches the charred, crumpled figure to her chest, rocking it slowly. There's a strange blankness to her face, as though she can't quite form tears, though she wants to.

I cry enough for the both of us when I finally make out what's in her arms. There's barely anything left of the mangled body. Just charred bits held together in a blackened dress, like burned potatoes in a sack. The figure doesn't appear human any longer. A tuft of black hair stands out pathetically on the scalp, still glossy in defiance of the body's destruction. A pair of bloodstained slippers hang off her singed feet. They're pretty satin, with double ties, the way I do them in the morning for her.

The slippers. The hair.

"No."

The whimpered denial escapes me involuntarily. Tears begin to pour down my cheeks.

No. No. It's not real. This can't be happening... But it is. It did. This was exactly what happened.

Neva.

The scary monsters mummy hid me from me got Neva.

Mummy lifts her head and the recrimination in her gaze makes me flinch.

"You told," she accuses. "Carmine, you told!"

"No," I say, shaking my head uselessly. "No, I didn't! I only told you!"

*"Liar," she hisses. "You told. And this is **your** fault."*

"My... fault?" I repeat the words as though they don't make sense to me. Truly, I reject them. I can't accept them... can't accept the fact that my sister's death is at my hands.

Neva is dead and it's my fault.

Someone... someone must have overheard me telling mother. It's the only rational explanation I can think. If I'd remained quiet, like sister had asked...

It is my fault. I have as good as killed her.

My fault, my fault, my fault...

When I drag myself out of the painful past and into the repellent present, I've seized fistfuls of my gown and am moments away from tearing the fabric to pieces. My eyes burn fiercely with the desire to cry. I can't breathe. Can't bring myself to look at anyone else at the table.

Uncle's punishment is subtle and effective. Most of the guests at the table haven't noticed what he's done. They remain completely oblivious to my Uncle's magic. Striking me with a psychic attack has more decorum than a physical blow.

I really prefer to be struck, if I'm honest. At least I see it coming. At least I know what to expect.

This was a favorite trick of mother's, to use the *Malaise* on me, or really, anyone who displeased her. It's not a concentrated attack, like the host of nightmares of which night hags are capable, but it strikes blindly as a smarting wound. And, of course, *this* is the memory that surfaces.

To most, it probably looks as though I've just tried to swallow my tongue.

"You were saying?" Uncle continues in a low, deadly voice.

"Nothing," I gasp at last. "Nothing. I... I need to retire, Uncle. I don't feel well."

Uncle's expression smooths into the non-threatening plainness to which I'm accustomed. After the attack he just lobbed at me? His expression rings false. Like calm waters with sharks swimming just beneath their surface. I shudder to think what he'll do to me if I anger him twice in one night.

"Of course, sweetling. Prince Achmed, would you mind asking your valet to escort the Princess to her room?"

"No need," I squeak, scrambling up from my chair. "I'll find my way."

I sway, truly dizzy.

Perhaps I *am* coming down with an ague. A sense of lassitude settles over me at once, almost pressing me flat to the floor. Still, I don't want the enigmatical Anon with me. I'll drag myself across the floor with my nails if I must. I need to be free of this room.

Staggering like a drunken sailor, I bypass the doors of the great hall. The second I'm out of sight, I get my wayward feet beneath me, kicking off the satin heels before running down the corridors like a hellhound nips at my heels.

THREE
CARMINE

My energy returns almost the instant I clear the dingy stone walls of the castle and burst into my gardens. It takes a few moments for my eyes to adjust to the darkness, but I don't need the faint silver shine of the moon to navigate my way. I know the garden path by heart, having walked it almost every day since I was old enough to do so.

I can't claim sole credit for its beauty. Much of the original framework was put into place before my birth by Neva's mother, the late Queen Camellia. She's buried near the arbor, under a row of roses. The beautiful blooms are just starting to open. What remained of Neva is buried nearby, under a thicket of white roses that are among the most carefully tended in my garden.

I twist my gloved hands together guiltily. My hands feel strangely sticky, the way they rarely do any longer. I've always had problems with sweaty palms, which my mother always attributed to acute anxiety. The sweats happen most often when I'm around people, which is why I'm so often in the gardens.

The garden metaphor is apt, I suppose. This ought to have been Camellia's space and Neva's birthright. Instead, I've come in like purple loosestrife, choking out the original heir with my selfishness, taking over the place that is rightfully hers.

Though I never intended to, never meant to. Had I the chance, I would absolutely resurrect Neva and place her back in her position of first heir. But, alas, such chances are simply wishes lost on shooting stars.

The night blooming jasmine perfumes the air, as does the lingering scent of roses, and the sickly sweet scent of the Drecaine vines that have begun to sprout and wind their way along the high garden walls. They're pleasant enough to smell and look at, but I don't dare touch them. Deadly poisonous, they have to be handled with the utmost of care. I'm not quite sure how they made their way in, as they ordinarily grow only in Wonderland. I don't question their presence here for long. Odd plants spring up in my garden now and then. I believe they are portentous of something—perhaps the fact that I may be a witch or perhaps one of my maids is. It would be an automatic death sentence, were Uncle to find out. So long as the vines stay on the walls, so long as they never escape this garden, there's no cause for worry.

The crisp evening air and familiarity of the place settles me, and I gain better footing the further I wander into my sanctuary. Perhaps it's best that Uncle struck me with his power and I sought refuge here. I need to visit Neva, to speak to her, though I know nothing but the wind will answer me.

Still, I reach out to her. To tell her how awful this situation is—that I don't want to leave. And I tell her how terrible Uncle is. And, of course, I apologize to her, such that I always do.

My Uncle only rules as regent because I haven't turned twenty yet. In mere months, I will be of age to rule in Ascor. He's only been permitted to rule in my stead because he's my blood. He is not, however, the *ruler* of Ascor. Ascor is not like Delorood, which has handed its rule over to a foreigner after both the King and his heir died suddenly. Noble or not, King Bastion ought not be on the throne.

I reach the arbor at last. It's a shady little alcove, climbing with yet more Drecaine vines. The wood is polished ebony and would blend almost seamlessly with the shadows, if not for the white blossoms that occasionally dot the vines. I've been trying to prune them before they bloom. Wonderland flowers talk and these vines are particularly ill-mannered.

"Whore," one of them hisses at me the instant I sit down.

My eyes wheel to find it. It's just a little thing, with a face barely peeking out from behind one lunate leaf. It's only just begun to bloom. The bushy stamen would tell me it's a male, even if the voice didn't.

I scowl up at it. "There's no need for name-calling."

"You pruned my brother, you whore," he hisses back. He's quite the rude bloom. "I'll call you what I like."

"If you continue to speak in such a way, I'll prune you too!"

The thing looks like it's scoffing at me. "If you don't want us here, you shouldn't summon us."

"I didn't summon you," I reply hotly, my melancholic preoccupation slipping a little in my anger. "And I wouldn't have to prune you if you wouldn't keep singing at all hours of night."

"Singing is what we do."

"Drinking songs and limericks?"

"Wouldn't need to sing for it if you'd give us some proper spirits."

"And what would I say to the king? The Drecaine vines want ale?" I laugh at the ridiculous thought.

"Cider," the rude vine corrects. "Don't want any of your human piss water."

"As if cider will go over better," I snort. "Now do be quiet before I find my shears."

"Whore," he mutters again before his petals curl inward once more and he falls silent.

I fist my hands into my skirts again, this time in frustration. The fabric slides through the gloves and I tug them off in frustration, throwing them to the ground. Sweat be damned, I want one evening where I don't have to wear the blasted things. Uncle can give me that, surely? If I'm to be married and sent off to Gods only know where for Gods only know what purpose, I can at least enjoy my last nights of freedom.

I pluck a pair of shears idly from their place beneath the bench in the arbor. Perhaps I should prune. Doing so will give me time to puzzle things out—to figure out what my next moves should be. And then I realize I'm only kidding myself—I have no next moves.

If Uncle sends me away, there's no one to rule my kingdom. No one except a regent. But why would Uncle do that? He has to know Ascor will not accept him. Unless...

Unless they have no other choice. Unless, like Delorood, a regent is the only option they are given.

My stomach bottoms out, like I've hit the zenith of a hill and have been pushed roughly over it, plunging down into uncertain waters below.

29

No... surely not! He's sending me away with Achmed, not handing me over like a pig for slaughter... There has to be another explanation.

There has to be!

Before I can examine this horrifying thought too thoroughly, however, I hear sounds from the other end of the garden. Someone is moving through the narrow garden path, and they aren't being careful about it. At least one of the saplings I've been tending snaps beneath a man's booted foot. I spin, so my back is to the wall, the bench braced behind my knees. Then I slip the shears into the corner, out of sight, but within reach if I need them.

I fold my hands primly in front of me and pretend to examine the new Camellia blooms.

I wait.

I don't have to pose for long. Two men round the corner a minute later. A quick peek in my periphery reveals it's Prince Achmed, closely trailed by Anon. Both stalk forward with almost predatory grace. Neither one of them can see me just yet, hidden as I am by the arbor shadows.

"You said it would work," Achmed hisses to his valet. "You said *Eversleep* should make her faint. Then I could have her before you do your business."

Bile creeps up my throat as his meaning registers. The dizziness I felt earlier wasn't stress. I was *drugged*! Achmed and his valet have been conspiring to rape me! Was that why Anon stood so confidently in my doorway earlier? He'd already made plans to defile me even then?

Neither knows that Draven has inured me to poisons and sleeping drafts for this very reason. The dizziness probably ought to have been a clue that something corrupt was going on. But I haven't had *Eversleep* in years.

I'm shaking with rage by the time Achmed and his valet come alongside the arbor. Anon seems surer on his feet than the Prince. Is he like me, perhaps? Something not quite human? My mother's night hag biology gives me an edge after dark, though I'm told my senses are pathetically dull otherwise. It's Anon who spots me, not Achmed, which solidifies my suspicions.

He's not human. Or at least, he's not wholly human.

I inch back toward the bench and my makeshift weapon. The smile Anon hoists onto his lips is seconds late and strained.

"Princess," he says in a faux jovial tone. "We are so glad to find you well. My Prince was concerned when you left so speedily."

I'm tired of playing this charade. "Because he might miss his chance to force himself upon me?" I spit back acidly.

31

The pair pauses for just an instant, exchanging a significant glance.

"So, you overheard, little eavesdropper," Achmed says.

"You must have inherited more from your mother than we anticipated," Anon continues. "Reports say you're not a night hag."

All geniality drains away from his face, replaced with an arrogance so cloying, it makes my stomach sick. Furthermore, I can smell the conceit upon him. Every emotion has a scent, though none are usually so strong I can scent them on skin. This man must be truly full of himself.

"I'm not a night hag," I insist. "And you're not half so subtle as you think."

Achmed carries on, either not hearing me or ignoring the jab. Behind him, Anon reaches into his cloak and withdraws a blade with a soft snick of sound. Human ears wouldn't register it. But I'm not wholly human either. Finally, fear seeps in and my anger fizzles and melts away like Sweetland's candied floss under rain.

Anon is armed and Achmed is reaching for me. I haven't truly escaped, after all. I'm backed into the arbor, with a stone wall at my back. I can't hope to climb it before one of them plucks me off. The arbor hems me in on both sides, with Achmed and Anon blocking the only other exit.

I'm trapped and at their mercy. And they have no mercy to offer.

Achmed wears the triumphant smile of a tiger as he sees the realization play out on my face. "Turn around and grip the bench, Princess," he says, voice silken and dangerous. "Play along and you can survive for a few weeks after the wedding. Who knows? Maybe I'll fake your death and take you across the desert to serve as my concubine. In a few years you can bear me a son. Your Uncle wants you gone one way or another."

"N… no. He doesn't…"

Uncle is all I have left in this world. My only family. How could he betray me like this?

"No, Achmed," Anon hisses. "It ends tonight. Fuck her if you like, but afterward, we have to stage the thing properly."

Achmed tuts as my stomach drops.

"You have no sense of adventure, Anon. Sure you don't want a chance at her? She's quite fetching. Wonder if the thatch on her mound is just as red as her hair?" He grins wickedly and licks his lips. "I suppose I'll soon find out."

He reaches out a hand to stroke one of the red ringlets that falls around my face. Sleek and blood red, it's one of the only hints to my heritage. That, and my silver-grey eyes. No human I've met has precisely the same color eyes or hair. Achmed runs his fingers along my cheek, grin widening when I flinch away from his touch. He skims his thumb very lightly over my lip, frowning when it comes away clean.

"Thought the flush of your lips might be lipstick, since your mother was such a painted little whore. Doesn't matter. Turn around, Princess. I won't ask nicely a third time."

I plant my feet firmly. I can't hope to defeat both of them. Not in this dress and not lacking weapons. But I refuse to lie back and whimper while this villain divests me of the virtue I've been saving for Draven. One open-palmed slap over his ear ought to knock him senseless. Then I can run. How far I'll get though? There's really no telling.

Achmed reaches for me. I pivot slightly and raise my hand, throwing it across his face. I put all the power I possess behind the blow, grateful I've stripped off my gloves. Now there's nothing to cushion the blow.

I strike the portion between his jaw and cheekbone. The second my sweaty palm makes contact with his skin, Achmed's eyes roll back in his head, showing only white.

Then he drops dead at my feet.

FOUR
CARMINE

For a second, I stare at Achmed's prone form, absurdly hoping he'll stand up and say this is some sort of jape being made at my expense. The threats, the aspersions about Uncle, dropping to the ground as though dead. I want all of this to be some sick prank.

But he's not breathing. Where my hand touched him, his skin runs with black toxin. I recognize the toxin vaguely from one of my botany lessons. It's taken from an extremely virulent flower, *Aconitum Curare,* an illegal splice between Wolfsbane and Curare. The toxin tends to only be utilized by huntsmen and assassins. My gaze drops in horror to my trembling fingers.

I killed him with just my *hand. That means...*

The sweaty patches that began to sprout on my palms as a young girl were never anxiety-induced. They were *poison.*

Gods, what if I'd taken the gloves off to touch Draven earlier in the day? I'd have killed him as surely as I've killed Achmed!

I catch a whimper of panic behind my teeth and try to wrangle my mounting terror. Oh Gods,

I've killed Achmed. A prince! I've killed a prince!
And I didn't meant to! He wasn't a good man and
perhaps someone should have done it, but I hadn't
intended to! I just wanted to escape him!

This is witchery, no doubt about it. If what
they said about Uncle is true, then I've just handed
him the excuse he needs to execute me. Other
countries are more casual about the use of magic
when done behind closed doors. The odd potion
here or love spell there aren't strictly punished in
other lands, unless the caster becomes too brazen
and starts practicing openly.

Not so in Ascor. The law is clear and my uncle,
and mother before him, enforce it with frightening
rigidity.

Suffer not a witch to live.

I have to flee. Now.

And then I remember I'm not alone.

Anon stares down at Achmed's body,
nonplussed for a protracted second before his gaze
flicks back up to me.

"I wondered," he mutters, more to himself than
to me. "It was a logical leap. You're sisters, after
all. But it was never said that blood was a factor in
the choosing. The other two Chosen aren't related.
I wonder..."

I can't make sense of his words. Sisters? I've
been an only child for years, after Neva's death.
Neva's remains lie beneath the row of white rose

bushes, if there's anything left of her after all this time.

I reach behind me for the pruning shears. I'm not sure what to think about this new, horrifying revelation about my hands. I don't know the limits of this newfound ability and don't care to test them. My poison may work only once, or may need time to refill. An intact blade will always stab.

Anon doesn't miss the motion and whips the blade from beneath his cloak. I get a very good look at the six-inch silver dagger, complete with its thick steel guard and crest depicting an enormous bird in flight. I recognize it at once.

"Gryphus," I breathe.

He's a Gryphus huntsman, which means this situation has become more perilous than I ever dreamed. He's no ordinary assassin or royal lickspittle. He's one of the most deadly creatures in all of Fantasia. And he's here to kill *me.*

Every spare scrap of knowledge I learned from Draven comes screaming into my mind. Always go for the kill shot with a huntsman. Never allow him up to hunt you again.

I scramble to get ahold of the shears and bring them down as quickly as I can, missing his heart entirely when he twists out of the way. The short blades *do* stick into his thigh, as he extends his left leg to kick me into the wall. No doubt to knock me out and slit my throat while I lay unconscious. The move earns me a respite, at least, and I seize on the opportunity, tripping over the hem of my dress as I sprint in the opposite direction.

With a grunt, the huntsman pulls the shears free from his thigh and drops them to the ground with a muted thump before he comes tearing after me. A quick glance over my shoulder tells me he's not far behind, his speed making up for lack of knowledge of the terrain.

I'm never going to escape him at this rate. And even if I do, where will I go? I'll be wanted for the death of Achmed. A witch and a murderess. Who will believe the Prince tried to rape me? There's no shelter in Ascor. No allies. No one to protect me...

No, that's a lie.

There is one man.

An injured, semi-mad man trapped in the bowels of the castle for a crime unknown. It's probably suicide if I attempt to free Draven. He's not strong enough to face another huntsman. But I don't see that I have another choice.

I trip in the garden entrance and realize I have to shorten my dress or I risk losing my footing over the material. I reach down and tear off at least two feet off the bottom of the dress.

Anon's blade whistles through the air above my head, a strike that would have parted my head from my shoulders had I been standing upright. I seize the fallen scrap of fabric, rubbing the slickness off my hands and onto the fabric before shoving the whole lot back toward Anon's face.

Anywhere the fabric touches him, angry boils erupt, pulsing black toxin into his skin. He doesn't drop like Achmed though. No doubt, like Draven, he's immune or at least resistant to many poisons.

"Bitch!"

He lunges for me again, but he's noticeably slower. I duck beneath this second swing and then dive for the stairs. Three flights of them lead down to the dungeon. I hesitate for a moment, considering the best way down. He'll likely push me down all three flights, if he catches up to me on the stairs. So that leaves...

I leap onto the banister and push off, the silken skirts aiding in the speedy slide downward. I feel dangerously unbalanced and dizzy as the floors go whipping past me at an incredible pace. Above me, the huntsman bellows his outrage. His feet slap the stairs as he makes a mad dash after me. A senseless giggle rises to my lips, but I press a hand to my mouth to stifle it. I'm not out of the woods yet. Far from it. I'm likely stumbling into the belly of the beast.

With almost no warning, the banister ends and I find myself tumbling down the last stair and onto the cold stone of the dungeon floor. I don't have time to catch myself and blood bursts inside my mouth, washing across my tongue and into the back of my throat. I gag, spit, and try to recover the breath I lost on impact before the huntsman is on me. He's close.

A soft cry escapes me as I try to move. The inside of my cheek feels raw and blood continues to pour into my mouth. Did I knock a tooth loose?

Pushing up to my knees, I crawl into the dim interior of the dungeon. The light from the few, small windows is gone and only soft, flickering pools of torchlight illuminate the corridor and the inhabitants of the cells. Ahead I can hear the mumbling of Ia, Draven's mad cellmate. She speaks about bears again. What is her obsession with bears, I wonder?

The blow must have harmed me more than I imagined, because I cannot seem to recover my balance enough to stand. Instead, I crawl like a whining babe through the dark, hoping something or someone stronger will leap out to save me. The tears begin to pour when I realize I can't even open the bars of Draven's cage. The copied key was taken from the pocket of my soiled red dress and placed inside a small hidden cubby beneath one of the loose stones in the wall. Even if I reach him, I can't free him.

Gods, I'm so stupid. I'm going to die feet away from the only man I've ever loved.

"Draven," I whisper as loudly as I dare. "Draven please wake up. I need your help."

Vain hope, that my valiant protector will put out an unlikely win at the eleventh hour. If he were strong enough to force the doors, he would have done so by now. His face appears in the gap between the bars and my shuffling crawl stops as I truly take him in.

Gods, my poor, beautiful Draven. What was done to him?

One eye is swollen shut, black with bruises that are only just beginning to heal. Angry burns litter his neck like love bites from Sol himself. His hair has been mostly burned away, leaving it many inches shorter than I remember. It's gone from shoulder length to ending just above his ears. He's inexpertly shorn most of it off so it's at least all one length.

"Carmine?" he croaks. "What are you doing down here? You've split your lip! What happened?"

I don't have time to answer, because the Gryphus huntsman lands on his feet with a loud smack on the stone, just yards behind me. He strolls into the first pool of torchlight with an arrogant, swaggering gait.

"Got you now," he says with a smirk. His gaze flicks to Draven and it graduates into a leer. "Ah, Corvid. I was hoping to get you as well. Perhaps the bratty princeling had it right. Perhaps I should..."

He crosses the distance between us quickly, stopping my progress by the simple action of stepping on the remainder of my skirts. Though I strain, I can't move forward. Anon hooks a booted foot beneath my skirts and flicks them up with a simple kick. I lose sight of Draven in a shower of silk and crinoline. I still hear the vicious curse he slings at the Gryphus huntsman as Anon finishes his sentiment.

"Have some fun, before I kill you both."

"Touch her and I'll pluck your eyes out, Gryphus," Draven hisses in a tone of cold fury that chills even me, and I'm not its intended target.

"If you could escape, you would have, crow," Anon taunts, echoing my earlier suspicion. "Sit and watch and perhaps I'll make her death painless."

I bat desperately at my skirts. I'll fall on his blade if I have to. I won't let him make my death a spectacle, just so he can taunt Draven.

And it's this last act of defiance that allows me to see what happens next. A pale shape swings down from the ceiling, emerging from the darkness like the wings of a dove. The shape descends on Anon with silent, deadly grace. A blade flashes in a neat snicker-snack.

Anon's head parts company with his shoulders.

FIVE
SABRE

The Gryphus Huntsman's body lists to the left, his head to the right. Both hit the ground at almost the same instant with muffled, meaty impacts.

I peer at the parts critically, though there's likely no cause for alarm. Not many living things survive decapitation, which is why it's a favored move among my kin. Head and heart. Even shifters can't live without them.

My muted light of my signet ring begins to dim, confirming my suspicions. The bastard's dead. His fate rests in the hands of a Shepherd now. Propriety demands we find one and hand his name over so retrieval is easier. Shepherds are drawn to death and will find him in the end, but it's common courtesy not to leave a body to bloat, both for the Shepherd and anyone who might come across it.

But for this scum? I'll make an exception.

Spyros deserves more than the corpse of his attack dog delivered to his doorstep and alerting a Shepherd will alert the bastard that Guild activity has gone on within his city, bringing down swift and deadly retribution.

I nudge the head to the side with one booted foot, grimacing when a hot sluice of blood washes over the leather. I do hate messy kills. This sort of thing tends to be more Titus' style.

Speaking of the conspicuous oaf...

Titus lumbers into sight, coming in from the opposite end of the dungeons, carrying the unconscious body of a guard over one shoulder.

"You're late," I say in a clipped tone, trying to hide my annoyance. This is not the time or place for a family squabble, no matter how dearly I wish to box his ears.

Titus' chin juts stubbornly, giving me that halfway petulant look he's mastered. Kassidy can mirror it perfectly, though it's more effective for her, given how she's a tiny, attractive woman. In my experience, a woman throws a pout at a man and he tends to buckle easily. On Titus? It just makes my fingers twitch with the need to punch him.

"Excuse the fuck out of me, brother," he drawls. "I thought we might want to free Draven. But if you think he's better off continuing to rot in the cell..."

I purse my lips.

"You could have just taken the keys from his belt after incapacitating him," I point out.

Titus' massive shoulder lifts the man a few inches as he shrugs. "Maybe. Thought I'd try employing a little of that ingenuity you're always preaching about."

"Ingenuity?"

He shrugs. "We put this man in Draven's manacles and we've earned ourselves at least an hour or two if he's tucked away in the back of the cell."

"You think someone won't be able to spot the difference between a headless man and Draven?"

"You think human eyes will spot the difference in this piss poor lighting?" Titus quips. "And we'll place his head in the proper spot. No one will tell the difference." He pauses. "At least for a while. Until the smell becomes intolerable."

I nod, because he has a point, loathe as I am to admit it. Titus occasionally shows he has a mind behind the bulging muscle. Two hours is more time than we need.

"You're Draven's brothers?" a small, feminine voice asks from behind us.

I pivot slightly to face her, still keeping my sword at the ready. Just because I can't spot a threat doesn't mean it's not there. I won't be comfortable even marginally relaxing my guard until we're clear of the Forest of No Return.

The woman behind us has to be the huntsman's mark, Princess Carmine Resia. At first, I can't make out much of her. She's still somewhat tangled in her dress, but when she finally bats the thing into submission, I get my first good glimpse and I finally get an inkling why the slip of a girl has been Draven's ongoing obsession for years.

She's a study in contrasts, like an artist with only bold, opposing colors on his pallet. Her skin is milky white, and escapes being ghastly pale by a fraction. Her full lips and lustrous hair are true crimson like a cardinal's feathers, not any of the orangey shades humans like to call red. Long, dark lashes frame eyes of a hypnotic mercury and the only indicator of her heritage I can see. They're startling even to me, someone who's met members of her kin before. I don't doubt she's been taught to keep them fixed on the ground.

They're not fixed there now. She's staring at me in mixed awe and fear, her slim body shaking. Frightened of me or the scum that called itself Anon Lagois? Both seem equally likely. I did just behead a man before her eyes. It's not something she encounters every day, I expect.

I turn fully to face her, sinking down on my haunches so I don't loom over her like some storybook villain and frighten her still further. Extending a hand to her, I attempt a smile. It's not a skill I exercise often, and feels brittle and false on my lips.

"I'm Sabre and you're safe now, Princess."

She stares at my hand wordlessly, as though she's frightened I may haul off and strike her with it. With a sickening lurch, I realize that's exactly what she expects.

If the kills were sanctioned by the higher authority, I'd find whoever has struck fear into this maid's heart and end them. Unfortunately, the signet ring has returned to mundane metal. There will be no vengeance killing tonight, it seems.

She shakes her head. "I can't touch you… without my gloves…"

"I don't," I start but Draven interrupts.

"She's right," Draven croaks. His head is propped against the bars for support.

That, in itself, is worrying. Of the three of us, Draven is perhaps the strongest. Not necessarily the most skilled. We've competed for that title for many years and we have no definitive answer yet. But he's the strongest, which is why he volunteered for this post in the first place. To protect Leon's daughters. To see him so weak he can't stand? It's a testament to just how badly he's hurt.

I don't say as much out loud, however. Proud bird he is, he'll puff up rather than allow us to help if we peck at this moment of weakness. I'd like to get of here in a timely manner, so I cut Titus off before he can make mention of it either.

"What do you mean?" I ask.

"Poisoned patches on her palms," Draven coughs out.

The princess pushes to her feet, most of her shock disappearing as she stalks over to the bars of the cage.

"You knew?" she demands. "You knew and you didn't say anything?"

Draven tilts his head, so he can stare bleakly up at her. "Do you truly think now is the time to have this argument, Princess?"

Princess Carmine drags her lip gently between her teeth in a manner so enticing, my cock twitches once with interest. The reaction is so surprising, I still for a moment, examining it.

I'm not a virgin. Choosier, certainly than Titus, who'll bury his dick in any woman who seems inclined to take it. Choosier even than Draven, who was much the same in his earlier days and only gained some sense of propriety as he aged. Now he only has eyes for the woman before me. I've been with perhaps... seven women in the forty years we've been alive. Perhaps that's why I can't stop staring at that full lower lip as she presses perfectly white teeth against it.

I nod to myself. Yes, that has to be it. It's time I found a woman to take the edge off. This woman is Draven's. She's staring at him with mingled frustration and adoration, which tells me she wants him too. If it weren't for the complicated nature of their arrangement, he'd have been bedding her already.

Yes, I will keep my distance.

"No, I suppose now is not a good time," she says, heaving a sigh.

She flicks a glance at Titus for the first time, examining his bulky physique speculatively. For some reason, that glance sends a prickle of jealousy over my skin. Just beneath the skin, my feathers twitch, the desire to puff in indignation rising in me. Titus? She can turn that look on him, but fears me? It seems rather unfair.

"Are you able to get the door open?" She asks Titus. "I had a key, but in all the confusion..."

Titus nods, letting the guard slide off his shoulder. The man lands hard, a groan sliding past his lips as he meets the ground, but he doesn't stir. Titus must have stuck him with tetrodotoxin to keep him still. Again, I have to admit I'm grudgingly impressed with Titus' initiative. He has a tendency to be flippant about rules, but he's not fucking around on this mission. I'm grateful. I don't have time to herd him like an errant fledgling.

Titus fishes the key ring from the guard's belt and finds the appropriate key in short order, slotting it in the lock. Draven doesn't have the strength to prop himself up and falls limply to the ground when the door is opened. Titus' reflexes are quick enough that he catches Draven before his head can knock against the stone.

Fuck. We need to find a healer and quickly. This is worse than I thought.

"Draven," the princess whispers, voice tight with worry.

"C'mon," Titus mutters, heaving Draven off the floor as if he weighs no more than a babe. "We need to be going. Do you have the princess, Sabre?"

I nod then step forward, offering the Princess my arm again.

"We need to leave, and it's faster if I carry you."

A shaky smile appears on her lovely lips. She truly is a beauty. "I suppose I have no choice then, do I?"

Another shape shambles out of the cell, startling me. It's a woman and she's pale and grimy, with hair the color of ash and eyes that are a shade of violet so dark, they almost appear black. She's wearing the tattered remnants of a dress that was once dark and sleek, but is now bunched and stiff with filth.

"No, child," she says in an absent, almost musical tone. "You don't have a choice. Can't fight destiny. Flies right to you, it does. Blue and brown and black, with pretty falling feathers."

Princess Carmine glances guiltily between me and the newcomer.

"She needs to come too," Carmine says, biting her lip again.

Damn. I wish she'd stop that. My cock is stirring again and my hands itch with the desire to cup her face and see just how soft those lips really are. Would she gasp, if I bit her lower lip?

"We can't take her. We were only sent for you and I can't carry two."

"It's wrong to leave her here to die," the princess argues. "She's in leave of her sense and I'm sure my uncle will kill her if he finds her alone in the cell."

I grind my teeth. We don't have time for diversions, but the princess' face is so achingly earnest, I feel my will crumble, just a little.

"I can fend for myself," the madwoman says, sounding more lucid now that she's out of her cage. "I'm stronger than I look."

"I doubt you can keep up with a huntsman," I scoff.

She smiles then, a flash of dazzling teeth. Mischief sparks in her dark eyes and glittering white orbs flares between her fingertips. Magic runs along my skin, itching as though I'm being swarmed by ants.

"It's a wager then," she says with a laugh. "Last one to the Forest of No Return catches supper."

SIX
CARMINE

I cling to Sabre's neck, winding my arms so tightly around him, I'm afraid he'll choke.

A squeak of terror is caught in my throat, but we're moving too fast for me to give voice to it. If I open my mouth, I'm sure I'll swallow a fly or mayhap a beetle.

Sabre insisted I put my hair up before we left, which made no sense at the time. Now that we're underway, I see the necessity. We're navigating Ascor at an astonishing speed, leaping from rooftop to rooftop like some sort of sprite. I expect the motion to draw the attention of every citizen in the city, but despite his speed, Sabre's footsteps don't make a sound as he runs the length of the roof and then launches himself to the next. My weight doesn't even seem to trouble him and he balances like a cat, even without the use of his arms.

He's not the man I want to be cradled against, but his arms around me are comforting, nonetheless. His chest is not as broad as Draven's, nor rippling with bulky muscle like Titus', but Sabre is strong. Held so close to him, I can feel how firm he is. Not an ounce of softness to this man. I dare a peek up at his face, instantly admiring it.

He's nothing short of a work of art. Closer to beautiful than handsome, the way Draven is. Sabre's face is sharp, smooth, pale skin stretched over haughty cheekbones. His nose is long and straight, mouth a little thin, but still intriguing. His eyes are a light brown, almost the color of caramel. His hair is snowy and as long as mine, his braid reaching his waist. A stripe of vivid blue streaks through it, shocking in contrast to the pale color. There's a feather tucked into the tail of it, held securely by a leather thong. It's the same blue as the stripe in his hair.

He's Draven's brother, which makes him a member of the Order of Corvid. He must be a Blue Jay.

When he glances down at me, his gaze settles on the pendant between my breasts for an instant. A large scarlet stone nestled into a gold setting. He tells me it will keep the worst of what the forest can do from my mind. My heart hammers harder at the thought. I'm being ferried from one nightmare to the next. I'm secretly hoping this is all a dream I'll soon wake from.

My uncle tried to have me killed.
Draven is dying.

I've killed a prince and am now, consequently, fleeing the city, self-exiling to save my own skin, leaving my people under the reign of a phoebtor tyrant.

It's possibly the worst scenario I can conceive of, short of the seals splitting and unleashing Morningstar on the world.

"Are you alright, Princess?" Sabre murmurs. His voice is soft and a little mesmerizing. Are all huntsmen so… charming?

Heat seeps into my face, no doubt dusting my cheeks pink. I'm a wicked girl. I belong in Ascor. I love Draven. So why can't I keep my gaze from Sabre?

"I'm fine," I mutter.

Sabre launches himself off of the last rooftop and within seconds, we're wading into tall grass, the poofs of fescue tickling my bare feet as we pass. I repress a giggle. This isn't the time. Laughter feels wrong, with Draven's life tipping precariously in the balance. Up ahead, the gnarled branches of the black oaks rake through the night sky, as if trying to claw their way from the ground and climb toward the heavens. Dense fog curls out from the treeline, as does a creeping sense of menace. I shudder, drawing my knees up in a childish attempt to get closer to Sabre.

I don't want to go inside the forest. I almost beg him to take us around, though the journey would take days that we don't have. My uncle is nothing if not thorough. Anon won't be the only avenue he'll have pursued to dispose of me.

"Brace yourself, Princess."

We clear the line of tall prairie grasses and then we're plunging into the fog, darting through the trees and the terror piles onto me. I squeeze my eyes shut as visions assault me, but it's no use. The scenes play out behind my eyes just as well as if I'd kept them open.

Screaming wind. Blood pulsing thick and hot behind my ears. That's all I can hear.

Vines wind around me, thick and poisonous. Fire begins to burn through my veins. Drecaine. They grip my throat, tightening like a noose.

The cold is so shocking, I can't draw breath. It flays the skin off me, leaving me raw and exposed to the elements. I try to scream to the dark void, but can't give voice to it. There's no air in my lungs. The vines drag me down to the ground, tethering me there as shapes begin to move in the darkness. Huge, beastly shapes.

A young woman sits idly by, watching me with pity in her gaze. She's cross-legged on the muddy turf, amber eyes assessing me. She's familiar, in a way. A fringe of curly ebony hair peeks out from beneath the hood of a royal blue cloak. Her lips are scarlet and her skin is the same translucent ivory as mine. She's hauntingly beautiful.

Skin white as snow, lips red as blood, and hair black as ebony. That was what her mother had wished for.

"Neva," I gasp, somehow managing to loosen my lungs from the stranglehold of the cold. "Neva, please help me!"

"You have to wake, Carmine," she whispers, her voice strained and faraway. "Wake and find me."

"But you're gone! To a place I can't follow."

"No," she says gently. "I'm not. Find me."

And then I make out the shapes behind her, and I do scream.

Dragons. One gold, another midnight blue, and the last an onyx that almost blends with the starless sky.

"Find me," she whispers.

And then I'm bolting upright, screaming so shrilly it hurts my throat.

Strong, calloused hands grip my shoulders and hold me fast, trying to still my frantic thrashing. I didn't realize I *was* thrashing until this moment. I jerk my chin up, somehow irrationally expecting to be face to face with a dragon.

No, just a huntsman, which is only marginally less frightening.

Titus loosens one hand to rub at his jaw, a sunny grin spreading across his face as he stares down at me. Somehow, despite the angry red mark my knuckles have left on the side of his face, he looks happy. The expression lights up his face, fills his eyes with a secret, boyish sort of joy. His eyes are strange though. A sort of... wine red, a shade or two removed from Anon's.

That thought sobers me at once and I edge away from him just a little.

"Huh. With those soft little hands, I didn't think you'd be up for defending yourself, Princess. Good to know you can throw a decent punch, if need be."

My cheeks flame with embarrassment and I drop my eyes to my hands. Sometime whilst I was unaware, someone had outfitted me with a new pair of gloves. These are leather riding gloves several sizes too large for me, but they'll do until I can find a better pair.

"Sorry," I mumble. "I didn't mean to hit you."

He shrugs, that easy grin only growing wider. "My little sister hits harder."

"Kassidy?" I venture.

Draven has talked about her in the past, always with a wistful smile that I secretly envied. I want to make him as happy as she does. But Kassidy is his family.

My heart throbs hard, creeping into my throat, choking me with the world of new possibilities now open to me. Am I truly a princess now? I have no throne, unless I can reclaim it from my uncle. That makes me…

I'm just a common woman now. And common women can marry common men. I give a rueful little shake of my head. No, that's not right. Draven's never been a 'common man'. But the possibility still exists. If I can somehow make him see… if he would have me… we could be together in every sense.

It's all I've ever wanted.

"Yeah," Titus says, oblivious to my hopeful revelation. "Though we tend to call her Goldy, what with the thick hedge of blonde hair she sports. You might get to meet her, someday. She'll be frantic when she learns what's happened to Draven."

Thoughts of a happy marriage to Draven are curtailed by the reminder of Draven's condition. I scramble onto my hands and knees, the shaking resuming but for an entirely different reason now. I climb to my feet, but my knees knock horribly, threatening to fold beneath me. Gods, how could I have forgotten for even an instant?

"Draven! Is he…"

Titus is on his feet in seconds, steadying me. I can't help but be momentarily sidetracked by the calloused texture of them, so warm against my skin.

I frown. Skin? The gown I escaped in was long-sleeved…

A glance down reveals the blue dress has suffered a catastrophic reshaping. The palace tailor would have a fit if she could see it now. The sleeves are cut away, leaving only short puffed caps over my shoulders, the middle torn open to expose my midriff, though I'm not entirely sure if I'm not to blame for that. And the skirts. Gods, the skirts! The majority of the bluebell-shaped skirt is gone, cut away inelegantly by a knife. It's scandalously short, hanging just above my knees, exposing the pale, slim expanse of my legs. Thank the Gods that my mother's genetics allow for very little hair growth on the body. The thought of Draven seeing my bare legs… More heat floods my face.

"He's going to pull through, thanks to that madwoman," Titus says, reminding me the madwoman is still with us. "It's a good thing you demanded she come along."

"Why?" I manage.

He shrugs. "She's some sort of witch, I think. Brewed foul-smelling potions and set to work on Draven as soon as we settled in the woods. His fever broke hours ago and the burns are almost gone. It's a damn miracle."

Some of the tightness in my chest loosens. Draven is healing. Thank the Gods. Just the thought of losing him brings stinging tears to my eyes. I blink them back, swallowing convulsively. My throat is almost glued shut, the relief so potent, it chokes me.

"I need to see him."

For the first time since waking, I glance around. We're at the edge of the wood, standing atop a hill that overlooks a shallow valley cradled between two very tall mountains. The stone is a deep grey that appears plum in this light. A dusting of snow covers the twin peaks. It's pretty. The thin strip of land between has been blackened and the smell of char still lingers in the air, though the firestorm that ravaged the land appears to have happened some time ago.

Only one structure still stands, untouched by the devastation. A tiny, thatched cottage.

The Lordell Mountains.

This is the place.

My mother met her end here.

"He's in the cottage."

"The cottage?"

Titus nods. "The woman is tending to him. Sabre lost the bet and he's off hunting for supper. I'll carry you, Princess. You look shaky."

The bet? I'm not sure which bet he references but I'm too exhausted to ask. That, and all I can think about is Draven. Seeing him with my own eyes—making sure he's truly safe.

Before I can protest, Titus has crossed over to me, sweeping my feet out from under me. Once again, I'm cradled in the arms of a strong, capable huntsman. Titus makes me a little nervous, with his incredible bulk. I feel like a twig, easily snapped.

The short skirt rides up, threatening to reveal my feminine bits. I blush furiously and wedge my hands between my thighs in a desperate attempt to preserve my modesty. What are these men doing to me? I don't think I've blushed so much in my life. I'm constantly flushed when around them, and I've known them for barely an hour. Well, at least Sabre and Titus, anyway.

Titus just laughs, settling into a loping stride that'll have us arriving at the cottage in minutes.

"Don't worry, Princess. I'm not going to ogle you. Draven will beat my face in."

"Oh," I say, not sure what else to say.

He chuckles again. "I'm sure it's lovely between your thighs, but if anyone's going to stare, it's Draven."

"Draven?" I repeat, frowning. "I don't understand."

Titus eyes me knowingly. "Come now."

"I don't!" I insist.

"He's had blue balls for fucking years, watching over you."

The heat in my face intensifies and I swear I'm going to combust. "You must be… confused. Draven doesn't think of me… that way."

Titus scoffs, his brows bobbing up to touch his hairline. He's got lovely hair. It's long, like Draven's used to be. Nowhere near the length Sabre keeps his, but similar in one respect. It's ash brown, with a streak of unnatural color sweeping through it, red, instead of blue.

"Are you fucking kidding me, girl?" Titus laughs another barrel sound. "Draven has worshiped the ground you walk on since you've been old enough to court. He's not had anyone else since taking the mission because he wants *you* so badly. I imagine he's tugged his cock to thoughts of you for years."

I really should tell Titus not to talk the way he does—he's really quite rude, especially considering I'm a princess. But I don't say anything. Maybe owing to the fact that I'm still shocked to hear the words. And maybe because… I like hearing the words.

But, no… it's not possible.

If Draven truly wanted me, why hasn't he ever said something? Can't he see how much I want him? If he truly desired me, he would have expressed it. We could have been making love for years! I've dreamed of him stealing into my bedchambers at night, catching me with my hand beneath my skirts, stroking myself to thoughts of him. Draven seizing my hand, licking my fingers clean with a wicked smirk before replacing them with his own. His fingers inside me, and then his manhood, taking me roughly, claiming me as his.

Desire clenches tight in my belly and I feel myself growing wet at the familiar daydream.

Titus sniffs the air delicately, then smirks. "You want him as well, I take it? Shame. I really hoped..."

But he doesn't elaborate further. I'm squirming with discomfort now, both from the shameful wetness seeping into my smallclothes and the fact that he can *smell* it. I bury my face in my hands, whimpering in embarrassment. Does that mean Draven can smell it too? Has he smelled the musky scent of my arousal? And if he has, how in the name of Avernus couldn't he have known? I'm wet every time I'm around him.

We reach the cottage at last, and Titus sets me gently on my feet. My steps are still shaky, thoughts of Draven making my knees weak. I brace my hand on the door frame to steady myself before taking a deep breath, then twist the knob and step inside.

The interior of the cottage is warm, with a fire already crackling in the grate. A black stew pot hangs over the fire, woefully dusty. The original owners haven't been here in a while. In the center of the room is an equally dusty table and little else. Not lavish decorators then.

The sound of voices draws my attention to a room just off the kitchen and I find myself walking toward it. The door is open and I burst through it, too eager to see Draven to care about politeness.

A gasp escapes me. Titus is right. The change is nothing short of miraculous.

Drave is sitting upright in bed, supporting his own weight with ease. He's shirtless, slightly dewed with sweat and I stare for several seconds. He's chiseled perfection, his pectorals firm, the abs so solid, it looks like you could bounce a spear off them. My desire returns tenfold and I almost crumple to my knees.

His burns have faded to a barely perceptible pink. The sores I felt on his body are gone. The cuts are puckered pink lines on his arms and face. The vivid purple bruising on his eye has faded to yellow green, the only blemish on an otherwise perfect profile.

I could kiss the mysterious woman. She's dragged him back from the edge of death and returned him mostly whole. If I ever regain the throne, I'll give her a hero's welcome into my kingdom.

Draven turns toward me, relief easing the stiffness in his body, a perfect smile alighting on those lush, kissable lips.

"Princess," he breathes. "Thank the Gods. I thought we might have lost you in the forest."

"Lost me in the forest?"

He nods. "You were screaming and then you went limp..."

"I had... a terrible nightmare," I said, trying to remember the particulars, but now the memories are faded.

"That's what the forest does... fills your head with ugliness." He takes a breath. "I am so happy to see you well. I've thought about little else."

My smile threatens to break my cheeks. But uncertainty creeps in on the coattails of my joy. This doesn't mean he loves me. He's been steadfast over the years, a loyal friend and confidant. I believe he loves me, yes, but his love is limited. I believe I'm nothing more than a ward to him— someone he protects because such is his job.

I cross over to the bed, climbing onto the narrow mattress with him. The dimensions are barely enough to hold us both, even though I tuck my knees up as close as the short skirt will allow. I press a gentle kiss to his cheek. It's all my faltering courage will allow me to do. "I am so glad to see you're well, Draven," I murmur.

He turns his head, his lips brushing my cheek, as well. My heart thuds hard against my ribs.

"Likewise, Princess."

Titus lumbers into the room after me, lounging arrogantly against the door frame. On any other man, I'd have found that posture irritating, but not Titus. He, and his brothers, have all earned a right to that arrogance.

"Told you," he says, giving Draven a pointed glance.

"Told her what?" Draven demands.

Titus smirks and says nothing. Draven doesn't have time to make more demands of him, as Sabre enters the room moments later, clutching the carcass of a coyote. His somber expression softens as he catches sight of Draven.

"Looks like you're healing up nicely. I thought we'd have to put you outside to be consumed by our smaller brothers."

"Like they'd touch him," Titus scoffs. "They have better taste than eating charred remains."

Draven's face creases into a ferocious scowl. "Oh, fuck off, Titus."

The vulgarity is so unexpected, it makes me jump.

Titus' smirk only broadens, filling his boyish face with an impish sort of charm. "Glad to have you back, brother. You wouldn't believe what's happened with Kassidy while you were gone."

Draven sits up a little straighter, eyes flying wide. "Is she…"

"Fear not," Titus says and waves away Draven's concern. "She accomplished her mission in the werebear compound. You won't believe how. She got fucking married to their nobility! All three of the heirs. King Leith and his cousins."

"Married? To the werebears?" Draven repeats, frowning. "A political move?"

Titus shakes his head. "No. For love. I've never seen the king so fucking happy."

Draven shakes his head incredulously. "Our little sister, Queen of the fucking bears!"

"I was sure she'd end up a spinster," Titus concurs. "Too headstrong to ever settle down permanently."

Sabre looks at Draven with interest. "I thought you already knew about Kassidy, given your message. Yet, you sound... surprised?"

"Message?" Draven repeats.

Sabre further frowns. "The missive you sent us. The timing was perfect—it saved Princess Carmine's life."

Draven shakes his head. "What missive? I didn't send anything to you. I haven't heard a thing but the castle gossip from the guards. What's happened to Kassidy?"

"She's Chosen," Ia pipes up, matter-of-factly.

All heads turn toward her, surprise and suspicion playing out on the brothers' faces.

"How the fuck do you know that?" Titus barks.

"Because I was there when she discovered her powers," Ia says, smiling softly. "Used them to leech the dark away. I owe her for that."

"What are you on about?" Titus demands. "Who the fuck are you?"

She purses her lips thoughtfully. "I'm not sure, to be honest. But I know the who I was. The goddess that fell from grace, seduced by a monster."

"Who?" Sabre asks.

She looks at him. "Harmonia. Then I was Discordia. Now, I am neither. Yet, I am both. It doesn't matter though now. Thanks to your foul-mouthed golden seraph, I am reborn, here to serve a purpose."

"And what's that purpose?" Titus asks.

"I'm going to help you find them, huntsman. The Chosen Ten. There are four already found."

"Three," Titus grits out, his face clouded over with irritation. "There are only three."

"Four," she says mildly. "The siren, the omnifarious, the thief and the poisoner." She fixes me with a chill stare as I feel my stomach drop.

"The poisoner?" I repeat.

"Welcome to the ranks of the Chosen, Princess Carmine."

SEVEN
DRAVEN

Blank shock creeps through my mind, blotting out rational thought.

Impossible.

If Carmine was chosen, I'd have known. There would have been signs. Yes, there are the poison patches on her palms, but they've been present for years. And I never really considered them as anything more than an anomaly. One in a thousand night hags has the genetic makeup for such. Once, a line of night hags bred with dark fae, resulting in the unique ability to produce toxin, poisoning the body as well as the mind. Neither Salome nor Spyros possess the ability though...

"That's not possible," Carmine says, her voice a light, feathery whisper. Her mercurial silver eyes swim with unshed tears.

Though I know I shouldn't touch her, I can't help myself. I hook an arm around her waist and pull her into my side. She's so incredibly fragile. She draws every protective instinct I have to the fore. This is what I'm built for. Hunting those who hurt the innocent. And if the woman is telling the truth—that she's Discordia—then she's one of the most vile monsters to ever plague Fantasia. It doesn't matter if the rumors are true. I don't care if Morningstar tainted her. It can't excuse the evil she's done. I should kill her here and now...

But... she saved my life and healed my battered body. And that means I owe her the chance to explain her tale, even if she's completely mad.

Carmine nestles her head in the crook of my shoulder, pressing her body against mine. I almost moan. This is closer than I've ever been allowed and it's fucking glorious. If we were alone, I'd take her face in my hands, and kiss away the tears slowly spilling down her cheeks. Until I reached her mouth, then I would claim it, tasting her until her breath became rough and shallow. I'd roll her beneath me on the bed and...

Fuck. It's not the time to be thinking about this. I'm hard already and only saved from discovery by the heavy blanket draped across my lap.

Furthermore, I can daydream all I like but I know the truth—even if I were alone with Carmine, I wouldn't act on my urges. Just like I've never acted on my urges—purely because she's a princess and I'm her protector. It wouldn't be right to treat her otherwise.

I can smell her arousal, her scent clinging to Titus like the sweetest of perfumes. Titus, Sabre and I have adopted each other as brothers—swore a fellowship of blood and vengeance and I'd happily lay down my life for him. But I fucking hate him at the moment. She wants him. She's wet for him in a way she's never been for me.

My thoughts are forced back to the situation unfolding.

Discordia... Harmonia... Ia, isn't finished. She gives Carmine a faint, supercilious smile and begins to recite in an almost sing-song voice.

"Nightshade, Hemlock, Aconite, the Queen of Poisons she shall be, and leach the life from a goddess, who taints the world tree."

I recognize the verse. I've had it memorized since the oracle spat it up years ago. I've come to hate it, since I've met precisely one Chosen and for years I assumed she was dead. I still don't know if Neva survived the battle with Lycaon.

"It's not possible," Carmine repeats, getting paler by the second. When she'd come in, she'd been rosy as a schoolgirl, no doubt due to her newest infatuation. Now, she's adopting an ashy shade that's almost akin to her sister's. "There would have been signs. Perhaps there is poison in my hands but that's witchery. I'm just Carmine. Just a girl."

Ia quirks an imperious brow. "You haven't noticed new... growths in your little bower, Princess?"

Carmine hesitates, and I tilt my head toward her, examining the look of dawning horror on her face. I watch her struggle to deny Ia's claims and when she can't, the look of bleak desperation steals in to take its place.

"Princess?" I prompt gently.

She burrows her way deeper into my side, as though by doing so, she can protect herself from Ia's chill stare. I wish I could save her from this. If it's true... Gods, if it's true, it means she's in more danger than even my worst nightmares have ever conjured. Forget failing to save her from a dirk in the back, if she's Chosen, she'll be a target for Morningstar, himself.

I have the grisly image of the giant winged form of Morningstar plucking Carmine from the ground like a wild rose and crushing her with ease. My body chills with an echo of her horror.

No. Never. I won't allow it. I'll die a thousand bloody deaths at Morningstar's hands before I let him lay so much as a finger on my Carmine.

"There have been... new growths," she admits. "I didn't think anything of them. I assumed... I assumed someone brought them in and planted them without consulting me. Or that perhaps they cropped up naturally."

"What were they?" Ia asks, still giving her a knowing smile.

"Drecaine vines and those rude Wonderland blossoms. One blossom called me a..."

Her cheeks color prettily. Gods I want to kiss her, want to rip the remnants of her dress right off her to see if the flush extends to the rest of her ivory skin if I were to spend the evening between her legs. I *do* like the fact that her dress has been shorn, even if Carmine seems uncomfortable. It's fucking incredible to feel so much of her bare body against mine.

"A what?"

She dips her chin a little, mortification stealing over her face. "It called me a whore," she whispers.

"I hope you plucked the little bastard," Sabre mutters.

It's the first time he's really spoken since Ia made her pronouncement. It's very Sabre to sit back and watch a confrontation play out until he can be sure of a course of action. The irritation in his voice is new. He's not prone to strong displays of emotion. My beast form shifts restlessly just beneath my skin, settling like I've just been spooked.

Does Carmine provoke this reaction in all huntsmen? I certainly hope not.

She lets out a breathless little laugh that sounds more like a gasp. "I would have tried, if there'd been time. Of course, you know what happened instead."

Once again, I find myself bristling, the beast rising to defend its territory. I've watched over the fledgling girl for years, watched her mature into a beautiful young woman. And *Sabre* is the one who effortlessly draws a laugh from her? No. Fuck no. I'm not going to let my brothers come in and steal her away. She's mine until she says otherwise.

It's not my place to make the request. Leon was a dear friend and I'm a bastard for lusting after his daughter. But I'll be thrice damned if I'll let one of my brothers waltz right in and take her without a fight.

Ia's smile warms, satisfied at last. "So you see?"

"It doesn't prove anything," Carmine says stubbornly, crossing her arms beneath her modest breasts, hoisting the swells just above the neckline of the dress. It's distracting as fuck.

"No, but this does," Ia says, reaching into the folds of what was once a black dress. She rummages before producing a perfectly round, crimson stone. She raises it to the light and, as we watch, it begins to glow a bright, sanguine color, like freshly spilled arterial blood.

Ia smooths a finger over it lovingly. "This amulet can detect the presence of a Chosen."

"Liar," Titus growls.

She tosses it to him and, on reflex, he catches it. He looks a little panicked. The first lesson that any child, shifter or not, is taught is not to take gifts from witches. Doing so always ends badly. He stares as the amulet as though he expects it to combust and scorch his hand off.

Nothing happens, except that the glow dies upon contact with his skin. After a second, he tosses it to Sabre, who catches it with equal ease and examines it more critically. While not necessarily a mage himself, he's our scholar. He can recognize enchantment when he sees it. He frowns, prods the amulet with a long finger and inspects the other side.

"It's not spelled," he says finally. "Dipped in something magical, but it's not a potion. I can't fucking tell what it is, except that it has the same chemical properties as blood."

"Precisely," Ia answers. "Morningstar's blood."

"What?" Titus echoes dully.

"You heard me, huntsman," Ia tuts. Then, when she takes stock of the room and sees the mirrored expressions of confusion and horror on our faces, she sighs.

"Get a stew going, Bluejay," she says scornfully to Sabre. "I can tell this is going to be a long night and I am starved."

We stare after her as she sweeps out of the room, out to the dusty kitchen and begins fiddling with the stew pot. We exchange glances with one another and, without any other options presenting themselves, we do the only thing we can.

We follow.

EIGHT
CARMINE

We're all gathered around the small, dusty table watching Ia bustle around the kitchen, making food. After chiding Sabre on his lack of culinary imagination, she'd swiped the carcasses from his hand and proceeded to make a meal of them. The first skinned carcass was diced and put into a thick stew while the second was cut into thick slabs and spiced, though I didn't know where in the world she'd scrounged the supplies from.

It was strange to watch her crouched over the sizzling meat, knowing who and what she once was. I'd not been old enough to *see* the true horrors she'd wreaked as Discordia, but I'd read about them in my history lessons. Uncle Spyros had seemed to have a special sort of reverence for the fear she struck into the heart of mortal men. Why hadn't she been a guest of honor of my Uncle's, instead of a condemned prisoner?

I can only guess it was because she was being truthful—she was no longer Discordia. But if she was no longer Morningstar's general... then what is she?

"You promised us an explanation, witch," Sabre says coolly from his perch on the window sill. Titus nods emphatically from his position by the door.

There were only three chairs set out at the table, which forced two of our number to stand or find alternate seating. The men had all but shouted me down when I suggested I lean against the wall and allow one of them to sit. Draven had been seated owing to his still healing injuries, and Ia took the third. Though they were all convinced she was evil incarnate, gallantry seemed so ingrained in their bones, it was reflex by now.

"And you shall have it, bluejay," she says, flipping the steak in the pan. "After dinner."

The sizzle of grease in the pan is comforting, like childhood afternoons in the kitchen, pestering the servants for stories. The cook and scullery maid used to be so kind and infinitely patient with Neva and I... But that had been before the sack of Ascor. Before my wagging tongue had brought the hellhounds to our doorstep to char my sister to ash and gut my father like a trout.

Tears prick my eyes.

Even now, so many years later.

"You'll tell us right fucking now," Titus growls. I can't help but feel just a tickle of desire at the deep, commanding bass of his voice.

Draven stiffens a little at my side, nostrils flaring subtly. My cheeks burn once more. Is Titus right? Can Draven truly scent my desire? It's mortifying, if so. Something cold flickers in his gaze, but I can't read it. Don't want to read it. If he's disgusted by me, I can't stand it.

Ia lifts her gaze from the pan. "It's easier to keep coherency when I'm well-fed and rested. I'm not myself and, if you'll pardon the crass speech, it's confusing as fuck. I can barely remember the last time I was Harmonia. I've been *her* for over fifteen years. I don't want to be her again, but she's all I know."

Then she casually picks a piece of the stewed meat from the pot, ignoring the searing broth. I can see the roiling from here and know the liquid has to be boiling hot. Her fingers only come away slightly pink. She pops the meat into her mouth, chews, and then lets out a long-suffering sigh.

"Explain," Sabre says.

"I will," Ia responds as she looks up at him. "And you'll have to forgive the gaps, you irascible curs."

She takes a deep, fortifying breath and lets it out slowly, her eyes sliding out of focus as she focuses them inward, on yesteryear.

"It was the battle of Osthedge, I believe. That pitiful little hamlet that lay just before the Anoka mountains and the desert around it. Morningstar destroyed it and lay in wait for the Guild attack with his retinue waiting in the wings. But he crucially underestimated Veles and his brood. Seven dragon sons..."

She gives a bitter shake of her head, pauses, frowns and confusion plays over her face, the bitterness of Discordia battling with her new priorities. After a second of contemplation, she shakes her head again, this time to clear it.

"Veles struck at Morningstar whilst they swarmed us, overwhelming us temporarily. The Blue Faerie's magic protected them for long enough to get the job done. Just a little longer and Veles might have claimed victory over his foe. He still managed to savage Morningstar's chest, one of his infernal claws grazing the general's heart. It spilled onto the bald face of the mountain and the loose stones at its base. The stuff that arced into the air was carried away by the zephyr wind, which whipped it to the corners of the earth, seeking out the worthy."

"The Chosen," Draven murmurs to himself. "You're saying Morningstar's blood marks the Chosen as his equals? That's why they'll be able to defeat him?"

"It gives the Chosen power, yes. But Morningstar knows that now. Blood calls to blood. All of Morningstar's strongest warriors have been given amulets for the express purpose of finding and eliminating any Chosen they encounter."

"Why are you no longer Discordia?" I ask.

Ia looks at me. "I'm in the Guild's debt for freeing me. That's why I'm telling you all of this." She faces the others again. "If Morningstar can easily detect the Chosen, he'll kill them all and end the battle before it begins. You have to destroy Bacchus' camp and steal the remaining stones."

The men stare at her and though they're so disparate in looks and temperament, they wear identical looks of horror.

Sabre is the first to react, sliding off his perch silently and striding purposefully toward the door. I catch a look of pure, unfettered rage on his normally stoic face and shudder. Somehow he's more frightening than bulky Titus.

When the shock fades, Titus looks uncharacteristically unguarded. It's an almost boyish look, and I want to cross over to him and brush his long hair from his eyes and assure him things will be alright. Before I can act on the thought, he, too, turns and walks out the door.

Draven remains still and silent, not moving but staring dead-eyed at the fire. It chills me more than the fleeing huntsmen ever could. Because in that moment, he's not *my* Draven. He's someone else, somewhere else, trapped in his mind.

"What's wrong, Draven?" I whisper. "Why did they go?"

"They're incredibly pissed, I expect," he says quietly. There's still a hint of rasp in his voice, and it seems thicker now. "They'll need time to calm down and think logically about this."

"Why?"

"Because," Draven says, swallowing convulsively. "Bacchus' revelry invaded our colony when we were ten years old. They pillaged, plundered, and raped before trampling everyone to death in one of their dances. We were the only survivors."

NINE
TITUS

None of us can sleep and it doesn't take long to reach a silent, mutual agreement.

We're going to do as the demented witch says, if for no other reason than to deliver much needed justice. It's the only exception we've ever agreed to make to the huntsmen code. We're going to kill the drunken son of a bitch who killed our families, whether the justice is sanctioned or not. Kill him and all of his attendants, down to the last maenad.

The coming confrontation has made all of us restless, even the witch, a fact which should truly scare us. If she's telling the truth, she's an evil force to be reckoned with, only overshadowed in might by the real heavy hitters, the six other generals handpicked by Morningstar, himself. If she's scared, I ought to be pissing myself.

But strangely? I'm not. My concern mostly centers around my brothers, especially Sabre, who I see very little of now. He stays in his jay form, flying above our heads, keeping a bird's-eye view of the terrain, ready to swoop down and peck the eyes from any attacker. Dusk is falling over the Enchanted Forest, the flaming reds and golds reflecting off the silver trees in a breathtaking fashion.

I've always liked it here. It's quiet and peaceful. Often fog-draped and cool, but dotted with hot springs to soothe the bite of the evening air. If I were ever to retire from this life, I'd come here and set up a territory. Fight the occasional monster. Maybe settle in and take a wife eventually. I'd be one of the few who ever did.

Huntsmen (and women) don't marry for a reason. It's dangerous to form attachments. And when we settle? We mate for life. Not a good idea in a line of work as dangerous as ours. Marry a huntsman or woman and you risk losing them to a mark they hunted. Marry a mortal? Be forever tethered to a vulnerability.

It drives Gatz half-mad that he can't have the tenacious Tenebris. He's long since turned his passion to lethal obsession.

I worried for Draven, once upon a time. Now that I've met the Princess? I can see her appeal. And with her powers, she's far from a helpless victim. She's actually perfect for him.

I can't help but envy Draven, just a little, though we all knew, of the three of us, he'd settle first.

Sabre's myopic, as sharp as his steel and just as cold. He makes killing a neat, utilitarian art form and has time for little but the relentless hunt. Me? I'm a self-admitted whoremonger.

My gaze wanders to the edge of the clearing where she sits, watching Draven stoke the fire, open tenderness in her eyes. She's besotted and the blind fucker can't (or won't) see it. I want to mash their faces together and make loud, obnoxious slurping sounds until they get the message. A fuck would do them both good.

And if he can't pluck up the stones to do it, someone should. He's my brother and I won't step on his toes to do it. Give him a fair shot. But if we survive and he's not done something about it? I'm going to do my level best to fuck her. Such a beauty should not be a maid.

She's too fucking tempting for her own good. The remains of her dress seem to disintegrate as we continue through the forest, the dangling threads catching on branches or brambles, unraveling the thing as we go. There's precious little of it left. The skirt barely covers her hips and rides up distractedly as we walk. Her ass is smaller than I typically like, but her hips are soft and round, and I can picture slinging her slender, shapely legs around my waist as I push my cock into her.

And the bodice? All but gone. I can make out the swells of her breasts over and under the thin band of blue cloth. Her midriff is bare, revealing an expanse of ivory skin that's flat but soft.

Unsurprising for a princess. I doubt she's done any manual labor. But it's enticing all the same. Would she squirm if I teased the underside of her breasts? Gasp if I lavished kisses and nips down past her navel and ripped the skirts away to reveal her soft mound? It's hard to tell with her smallclothes in the way, but I'll bet a gold coin she's got a thatch of scarlet hair to match the softly waving stuff on her head.

She's painted gold now too, the fading light almost reflecting off her pale, narrow shoulders. She's a goddess. Someone should lay her down and worship her like one.

It won't be Draven. Not tonight, anyway. He's taken one of the three bedrolls we were able to find at the cottage. Proud bird he is, he's trying not to show the fatigue he's feeling. He's almost whole, but the brews Ia gave him manipulated his life force, turning what should have been months or years of healing into an overnight cure. The cost is reduced energy. A trade-off I'll take any day. At least he's alive.

Saccharine Carmine tries to tuck him in and kisses his forehead when he's sound asleep.

I tear my gaze away when she glances up at me and catches me watching her. Hopefully she'll sleep and I can slip away to take care of my... substantial problem. If my cock gets any harder, it'll be painful.

The clearing is silent for a long stretch and I adjust myself discreetly, deciding it's about time to take my leave. With thoughts of her? It shouldn't take long. I won't leave them unguarded for long.

And that's when Carmine settles at the base of the tree where I've been situated, cleaning my weapons. It's comforting and keeps the worst of the rage from eating at my thoughts. It won't keep the nightmares at bay, but that's a problem for another day. I'm on watch tonight.

The sweet scent of her stirs the air around me. I can't pin down the scent. Magnolias? Lilacs? Jasmine? Roses? It would be fitting, given her surname. The Resia family is distant cousins to the viciously slaughtered Roses in their far-flung kingdom. But rose… that's not it either. It's like stepping into a flower garden, a scent so befuddling, all I can do is bask in it, trying to puzzle it out.

And her arousal? Fuck, it's even sweeter. The most fragrant perfume I've ever scented. I want a chance between those legs just to see what she tastes like.

"I feel awful," she says softly, taking me by surprise. She keeps her eyes trained sheepishly on her slippered feet.

"Not surprised. It's cold and you're not wearing much."

After a moment's thought, I peel my shirt off and offer it to her. It's thickly woven, designed to ward off arrows and daggers. It's too warm for me, most days.

She stares at it, pink dusting her cheeks. "That's not what I meant."

"Still true," I point out. "Put it on, Princess." I look down to her chest and can't help myself. "Your nipples could cut glass."

She gasps, her mouth popping open in shock. Her legs clench together on reflex as the frank but slightly filthy comment hits home. Her nipples pucker further under my scrutiny.

"That's... incredibly crude!" she says as she stares up at me.

"Nah. Crude would be saying your tits look absolutely lickable. You ought to let Draven do that sometime. Poor bastard's probably ready to bust a nut staring at you in that getup all this time. We're going to have to get you proper clothing when we reach civilization or his balls will drop off."

The flush spreads further, creeping down her neck and warming the tops of her breasts. More arousal perfumes the air. "You shouldn't... you shouldn't talk that way."

"Why?" I demand as I stare at her. My cock is officially, painfully hard. It's taking all my will not to seize her, kiss the breath out of her and drag her down to the ground for some good old-fashioned rutting. "It's the truth."

"I'm not so sure," she mumbles. "And even so… you shouldn't say… such things."

"Then why are you so turned on?"

"I'm not," she insists.

I chuckle. "I can smell your heat on the air."

Would Draven mind it so much, if I wait my turn? I've heard tales of the late huntswoman Peregrine who was shared among seven dragons. Could Draven share? Would he let me teach this slip of a woman the meaning of ecstasy? There's no man alive who can do breastplay the way I can. It's a fucking gift. One I'd love to give her.

She swats my bicep and it's a pitiful attempt, like the mere brush of a butterfly's wings, any brief sting it might have had stolen by the thick layer of her gloves. Someone needs to teach her how to throw a punch. Chosen or not, she can't be prancing around Fantasia too attractive for her own good and unable to defend herself properly.

"You're a… a beast!"

My smile is brief and full of mischief. She's easy to rile. I don't think I can recall being quite so amused in the last decade or so, with Draven and Kassidy gone and only sourpuss Sabre for company.

"Yeah, that's sort of the point."

She purses her lips, not willing to concede defeat and drops her facade of prim manners to insult me further. Does she know any curse words? She'll need schooling. It'd be entertaining to hear the word *fuck* fall from those pretty lips.

Especially if I'm inside her.

Fuck, Titus, get ahold of yourself.

"That's not what I meant," Carmine continues. The wind picks up and she finally gives up her fight against propriety, slipping my shirt on over the remnants of her clothes.

It's so large, it swallows her slim frame whole, looking more like a shift dress than a shirt. Give her a belt to accentuate her waist and it wouldn't look half bad. I reach for mine and her cheeks turn positively ruddy.

"I don't need your pants too!" she gasps.

I can't help the rumbling belly laugh. It's loud enough, I'm afraid it'll wake Draven or drag Sabre back to investigate.

"Calm yourself, Princess. I'm not taking my pants off, just giving you the belt to secure the shirt around your middle. Can't give you my pants. I'm not wearing anything beneath them and I doubt you want me to stroll about with my cock swinging about. If you want to see it, you'll have to ask nicely."

The Princess' mouth works like a caught fish, too shocked to even draw in a full breath. "You arrogant..." she starts, but can't seem to find the right word.

"Prick? Cock? Bastard? Rouge? Cur? Son of a bitch? Pick one, Princess, they'll all do."

"How can you speak like that?" she hisses, snatching the belt from my hands, wrapping it around her middle quickly before cinching it at her waist. "You don't know me! And, yet, you let your tongue run wild and say the worst things!"

"You don't have to know someone to fuck them, Princess. It's just nicer if you do. And I say so because you're beautiful. And as for my tongue? It's built to be between a woman's thighs or latched onto a woman's breast. When I'm not telling it like I fucking see it, that is."

Without my conscious permission my hand moves, brushing one of her nipples that still manages to show beneath the heavy fabric. She bucks in surprise and a soft moan gets caught in her throat. Her thighs quiver, the scent of arousal punching through the night air. Not for Draven this time. For me. My beast stirs, pleased, urging me further. But I've made my point. I let the hand drop.

She squirms away from me just a little. "I came over here to apologize, you brute."

"For what?"

"Monopolizing the bedroll. I wanted to tell you to take it when your watch is over. I hate that you and Sabre are constantly uncomfortable."

"We're not."

"But you're always sleeping against a tree."

"It's not uncomfortable and we can be stealthy that way. Find an Aspen and the dense leaves will cover even a bird shifter roosting in the branches. Trust me, Princess, we've had worse perches."

Her gaze whips up to the trees. "Is that where Sabre is now?" she asks, searching for the blue-white shape of him. He's not up there, and I'm grateful. If he heard half of what I'm saying to Draven's lady, he'd box my ears, just the same as he does Kassidy. It fucking hurts.

"Why is he so... distant?" she asks.

"What do you mean?"

She shrugs. "He looked dispassionate before, but ever since the cottage... I feel like I've upset him."

"He's not upset. He's angry. We're fucking pissed we didn't know about Bacchus sooner. We swore an oath to kill him."

"Then Sabre's..."

"Chewing on the horrifying thought that Bacchus is destroying more cities, stealing more lives and we haven't been there to stop it. Sabre... had it worse than me. His whole family's gone.

Mine isn't. I've still got living cousins, even if we don't speak."

"Why don't you speak?"

I pause. I don't like getting into this. Even if my brothers already know my filthy secret, we rarely speak it out loud. I keep my fears to myself, the fear that the evil is within me too and one day *I'll* be the one who needs to be cut down. Blood will out.

"If you want that story, you're going to have to do something for me."

"What?" she asks, instantly suspicious. Smart girl.

"It's embarrassing and I don't speak of it to outsiders. You want to hear the story? I want you to make a concession for me."

"What concession?"

"For the duration of the story, touch yourself. And when you're through, give me your hand. Don't wipe it clean. I want to see your juices."

She stares at me in open-mouthed shock again. Her cheeks are as red as her hair now. I realize then that she doesn't know what I mean.

"I can show you how," I say with a smirk. "It's easy when you get the rhythm."

Her mouth snaps shut and she glares her defiance at me. "I know how to do it!"

Ah, so I was wrong. It's my turn to be shocked, though the shock wears off quickly. The maid is saucier than I thought.

"What do you think about when you pleasure yourself, Princess? Tell me your tale and I'll tell you mine. What had you writhing in the sheets at night?"

For an instant, I'm certain she's going to tell me no. Crawl back to her bedroll radiating disgust and tattle on me to Draven in the morning. She surprises me again.

"I think of Draven," she murmurs. "Of him... catching me in my chambers, moaning his name. That he'll take my hand and..."

"Touch you?" I venture. "Finger fuck you to orgasm and then take you in any position he pleases?"

"Yes," she breathes.

I lean in. "Touch yourself for me, Princess. Spread your legs and let me see your pretty pussy while you moan his name."

I hope Draven is listening to every fucking word of this. No dancing around the idea she wants him now. Fuck, I wish I were the center of those fantasies. He's the luckiest bastard in all of Fantasia.

The Princess mulls my words over for a few seconds and then, to my surprise, removes one glove, slides her dress up, hooking her long fingers into the waistband of her smallclothes, drawing them down her shapely legs. What I see between those legs knocks the breath out me and I'm suddenly containing a moan of my own.

She's bare, as hairless as her legs. I know that can happen sometimes with night hags. But aside from her eyes and the smoothness of her skin, she doesn't look like a night hag. She looks like a damn work of art. Her pussy glistens in the last rays of the setting sun. It's fucking mesmerizing to watch her part her folds and expertly find that little bud at the apex, stroking herself lightly. She does this often, to know that place so intimately. I've met whores who don't know to manipulate their clit so skillfully.

Her head rocks back a little and her back arches. She makes a soft, pleased sound. Gods, maybe this was a bad idea. I'm already straining my self-control as it is. I'm going to cum in my pants like a fumbling teen at this rate.

"The story," she prompts in a breathy voice.

I'm suddenly self-conscious. What the fuck is she doing to me? I'm not a shy man. I decide to start with an easy question. "Do you know what bird I am when I shift, Princess?"

She frowns and examines me properly, scanning my face with more than professional interest, pausing her ministrations for a moment. At a pointed glance, she resumes, letting out a soft moan.

"No, I... ooh... suppose I don't. I know Draven is a..." Another protracted moan, drawing out Draven's name. So easy to picture him driving into her, drawing those sounds. I'd kill to watch it. To have her instead. Or fuck, to have her jointly. Anything. So long as I can watch or participate.

"He's a raven," she manages to gasp. "Sabre is a jay. I've never seen a Corvid bird with brown and red markings."

"That's because there aren't any." I swallow convulsively. Gods, I can't look away from her. "I don't know what my bird shape is either. I'm a bastard half-breed. Orders of Aves don't ordinarily mix. I shouldn't exist. And I fucking hate the other half. When most people ask, I tell them Order Accipitrine. They assume I'm a red-tailed hawk."

"But that's not true, is it, Titus?"

This time my name comes out on a moan. Fuck, fuck, fuck. I should tell her to stop. At this rate, I'm going to slip inside her and Draven will never forgive me for it.

"No. It's worse than that. My grandfather was a Gryphus huntsman."

She stops, stares, and then resumes. "I... ahhh... see. You're worried about facing your cousins."

"Gatz in particular. He threw in with Morningstar, led the whole fucking faction to get one woman. Belle Tenebris. He'll be with them. He's in love. It's why I'm a foul little whoremonger, Princess. I don't risk falling in love. A fuck is all I can ever give." I take a breath. "That's my story. You can stop, if you wish."

But she doesn't. Can't seem to, at this point. She arches her back, thrusting those small, perky tits forward and rolls her hips desperately, moaning Draven's name. She's lost to the fantasy and Gods, it's fucking nice to watch, even if it's not my name.

And then she's coming, a little breathless scream coming from her. I slap a hand over her mouth to muffle the sound. Can't wake Draven or give our position away. She shivers beneath my hands, then, to my shock, uses the hand not on her pussy to take my free hand and shove it into her hair. Getting the picture, I pull it tight, giving her an edge of pain with her pleasure. She bucks her hips against me, her warmth maddening against my thigh.

One thrust of her hips gives her enough friction and then she's at it again, bowing under the force of another, more intense orgasm. I can't help it. I remove my hand, instead swallowing the fresh moan in my mouth, tasting her sweet lips.

Her eyes are half-lidded and glazed with pleasure when I pull away and release my grip on her hair.

Where did this woman come from? She barely resembles the shy, unassuming Princess I just met. Out of bed, she's a nervous, twitchy thing. In it? She's a Queen, demanding what she wants.

She lifts the hand to show me the juices that glisten on her fingers. I take her wrist gingerly, avoiding the poisoned patches on her palms. Then I lick each finger clean, watching her face as I taste her.

Good. So fucking good.

My cock is painfully hard, demanding I slide into her.

Her blush returns and she squirms, still half on my lap. The question slips out before I can stop it.

"Do you want more, Princess? Do you want me to fuck you?"

I don't hear the answer, though. Because the shrill call of a jay splits the night, giving me a crucial second's warning before I hear the tell-tale sound of an arrow splitting the night air. Without thought, I seize the Princess by the waist and drag her twenty feet in the opposite direction. A crossbow bolt sticks in the tree, precisely where her head would have been moments before.

Then another hits, closer, just shy of my boot. No time for delicacy. I kick Draven lightly in the ribs. He rouses with a sound of protest.

"Up!" I shout at him. "We're under attack."

TEN
CARMINE

The shaft of an arrow comes to a quivering halt in the trunk of a tree very near my head. I stare at it for a stunned half-second as it stills, my breath catching in my throat.

Someone is trying to kill me.

Titus' bulk crushes me into the tree. I have to brace my hands against his back to keep him from pressing me flat as a flower against the trunk of an aspen. I'm momentarily distracted by the corded muscle of his back against my fingertips. Gods, there's no trace of fat on any of them, is there? Will Draven look as delicious out of his clothes?

The stunned second passes and I yank my hands away from his skin with a yelp, remembering the patches on my bare palm. Being speared through the heart with an arrow is an easy death when juxtaposed with any number of toxins that could reside in my flesh. It was much, much easier when I believed the patches on my hands to be unattractive sweat spots.

Draven comes alive with a thick sound of protest. He shakes off the stupor quickly when another spear comes flying into the clearing. In a move that's hard to track, he's on his feet, seizing the spear from midair, and launching it back in the direction in which it came. The dark shape that stepped into the clearing topples.

He casts a glance around the clearing, panic clear on his face when he can't immediately locate me.

"Carmine! Is she…"

"Got her," Titus grunts, stooping low to avoid another crossbow bolt. "Make yourself fucking useful and get my scythe. They jumped us while I was cleaning my weapons."

Draven doesn't question him, just lopes across the clearing, casually gutting the next man to step into the clearing. His eyes fix for a second on my abandoned glove and smallclothes, the muscles around his mouth and eyes tightening infinitesimally. He shelves whatever he's feeling and stoops to retrieve one of the many sharp implements Titus had been occupied with before my interruption and the following interlude.

The very, very inappropriate interlude. I still can't believe I took his bargain. Had I truly needed to know his past so badly?

Yes... or maybe... I simply wanted someone, *anyone* to speak to me as a woman, not a little girl who needs protecting. I know I can at least count on Titus for that. Of the three, he's come closest to treating me as I wish to be treated. As a common

woman who can do her own thinking and doesn't
need to be coddled. All my life I've been told what
to say, what to wear, who to court.

Taboo as it was watching Titus watching me...
it was also freeing. The undisguised want in his
eyes... it was exhilarating. If I'd said yes, Titus
would have entered me. I'm sure of it.

Draven whips a weapon toward Titus, and he
catches it easily, fingers curling lovingly around
the polished oak handle. There's a sound like the
peal of discordant bells as the rest of the weapon
settles, chain links settling in loops like a lazily
coiled snake. The wickedly curved tip of a scythe
bites into the ground a few feet away from us. Titus
jerks it up from the ground without effort, swinging
the scythe around as more bodies spill into the
clearing.

I watch in horror as the blade slices with ease
through the necks of several men, sending their
heads toppling from their bodies like popped corks.
Blood spurts from the severed necks in a fountain
of gore before they list sideways, their legs folding
easily.

There are more men coming, but I can't stop
staring as blood runs from the severed necks of the
men Titus killed. The thick scarlet pools grow
wider and wider, sinking into the packed earth at
last, as the ground absorbs the liquid offered.
Nature is a cruel mistress and doesn't truly care

what waters her garden. I've known that in theory.
But watching it play out in practice is another thing
entirely.

I need to move, need to make myself useful,
but I can't seem to unlock my frozen limbs. What
sort of Chosen one am I if I can't defend myself or
the ones I love?

There has to be some mistake. There's no way
fate can thrust this responsibly in my weak,
shaking hands. I'm not built for this! I'm not! I'm
just Carmine. I was never meant to be anything
more than the spare heir. And now with Uncle at
the helm? I'm not even that.

The shout draws the attention of several nearby
men to where Titus and I stand. Now that he's
given me space, I recognize the sigils on their
armor. These are men at arms from Ascor, trained
to guard my mother and then, after she perished,
my uncle. Now they're made to be my killers.

The leaves above us rustle and then an
enormous shape emerges from the bottommost
boughs of the aspen, sending leaves tumbling down
in a verdant rain between us and the line of
attackers. I can't make sense of what I'm seeing
until the shape alights on the ground, spreading its
magnificent wings wide. I blink at it in shock.

"Sabre, nice of you to join us," Titus grumbles.

It's one thing to *know* these men can turn into ravens and rooks and the like. It's another thing to *see* it.

Sabre's plumage is nothing short of magnificent. It's the purest blue I've ever seen, like the azure of a perfect, cloudless summer day. It's only broken up by dark stripes of black here and there, delineating subtle shifts in color that make up his pigmentation. His breast is snowy white, his head crowned with more ebony. And he's enormous—a bird the size of an elephant.

Sabre extends a wing toward me, shifting it impatiently in a sort of "come on" gesture. Titus gives me a shove toward him.

"Time to go, Princess."

I balk, planting my feet still more firmly. "No! I can't leave you and Draven here. And what about Ia? She's still recovering. We can't…"

"We're grown men, Princess," Titus snaps, swinging the scythe back into his grip. It's slathered in crimson and a few flecks fly off the blade to pelt my cheek. I flinch away from the warm spray. "You're the one who needs protecting. Get out of here and make our jobs easier!"

I don't think he says it to be cruel. He doesn't seem like a man who is cruel on purpose. Still, the words cut at me like a blade and I drop my eyes to the ground to disguise the tears that spring up.

Stupid, useless Carmine, crying at a time like this. Titus is right. I'm no good here.

I keep my face down, stumbling toward Sabre, kicking off my slippers, shoving them under one arm as I attempt to climb the proffered wing. The sensation is strange beneath my hands and feet. The feathers are glossy, almost slippery, and I slide a few times as I try to ascend to his back. I can feel the fine bones beneath his skin and feathers and I use them like rungs to hoist me toward the dip between his wings. He's easily twice as large as my mare at the castle.

It can't take more than a minute or so, but every second is fraught with peril and anxiety. Arrows whiz past my ears and I curse my plodding pace. I'm putting Sabre in danger too. Finally I settle between the dip of his wings, shoving my hand beneath the nearest row of feathers and hold on for dear life. More guilt hammers me when Sabre makes an uncomfortable sound in the back of his throat. I'm hurting him.

He doesn't give me much time to rectify the situation, though, because in the next instant, he's lifted us from the ground with one flap of his wide wings.

I squeal in surprise, clutch even tighter at the shafts of the feathers, and feel another stab of guilt as Sabre shifts uncomfortably beneath me.

It takes me a few seconds to loosen my fingers and settle myself on his back. The rocking motion isn't helping my rapidly increasing sense of nausea. My fingers feel numb. I can't help a small, breathless scream when the many reaching branches of the aspen rake at me on our way past. Warm beads start to roll down my face and I know I must be dripping blood down onto Sabre and what remains of my clothing.

I want to scream out loud again. Why this? Why now? Why *me?*

With a caw of defiance, Sabre bursts through the treetops and into the open air. For a second, I forget my screaming panic, I forget the painful scratches on my face, I forget how wretched I feel, because what I'm looking at is incredible.

The whole of the Enchanted Forest lays splayed out beneath us as Sabre takes us higher and higher. The silver cast of the leaves reflects back the blazing light of the stars, so that it feels like we're gliding in the misty middle between the stars and an inky, rippling ocean. The wind that whips at my face is harsh, cool, and tugs fresh tears from my eyes, but for just a moment, I'm not afraid.

The moment is short-lived.

A dark, slim shape slices the air with a hiss as it arcs through the trees and strikes Sabre's wing. The sound that escapes him pierces my heart, sending empathetic pain spider webbing through my chest as if it were I, not he, that had been struck.

We lose altitude almost at once, listing sideways violently. Sabre squawks, trying vainly to move the wing, but it's pinned in place, like a moth to a board. The remaining wing flaps harder, trying to make up for the loss, but it's no use.

We plummet toward the trees, and the journey through the branches is worse when done in reverse. I topple off his back, only just catching onto the tip of his good wing. The feathers strain, and I'm afraid the pair I'm gripping will come loose, dropping me to the ground below.

Sabre flips so his back is toward the ground, when it becomes clear we're doomed to crash. He jerks me in, toward his body, folds his good wing around me, securing me against his chest as best he can without fingers to grip me. The feathery embrace is warm, the brush against my cheek almost ticklish. Wind screams in my ears as we plummet.

It feels like we strike every branch on the way down. I'm shielded from the worst of it by his wings. I hear more crunches, still more tears squeezing from my eyes when an agonized moan sounds from Sabre's throat. I hadn't known his beast form was capable of making such a sound.

When we impact, almost a mile away from the campsite by my crude estimation, the landing rattles even my bones. Cushioned as I am by Sabre's body, I can only imagine how much worse it must be for him.

His grip on me loosens, his wing rolling out flat as his muscles go lax. I freeze to the spot in horror, watching his prone body. For one terrifying instant, I think he's dead. But, then I see the subtle rise and fall of his chest. He's still alive. Thank the Gods.

I can hear the thud of many footsteps as our attackers rush us. Too many to only be Titus and Draven. Are they dead? Have I condemned the three brave huntsmen to death merely by being in proximity?

A howl of anguish batters inside my chest, demanding release.

Draven, dead? No, no, no! I never told him the truth about how I feel!

I hammer the packed earth with a fist, pouring all my rage and despair into the ground.

A vividly purple bloom springs from the earth, spreading its petals wide as I watch in fascination. I recognize it at once. *Atropa Belladonna.* Deadly nightshade. A few have been cropping up in my gardens. I assumed someone had planted them for me to elevate my mood. Mother forbade them for years.

Can Ia's mad assertion possibly be true? Am I somehow one of the fabled Chosen? What could have possessed Zephyr to choose a weakling like me?

True or not, I have to try. They're so close now. Sabre can't defend himself in this state. He hasn't even shifted back to his human form yet.

I strike the ground again and again, almost in time with the frantic beating of my heart.

And it works.

Shoots, stems, and blooms spring from the ground in accelerated growth, rolling forth like a poisonous, colorful wave toward the men who've burst through the trees ahead. The vines part when they reach Sabre's prone body, forming a little grove around him. The eye in the center of a deadly storm.

Drecaine vines loop around our attackers' feet, rooting them to the spot as the tide washes in. Blooms pop along the vines, little faces appearing as the petals part and, as I watch, they lunge for any exposed skin, sinking stiff pistils and stamens into exposed flesh, oozing greenish poison.

Inhuman shrieks claw at my ears as puss foams from the wounds, agony contorts their faces, and their knees buckle. They topple sideways like the tin soldiers Neva once played with and are engulfed by the rest of the fatal flora.

Silence falls thick in the clearing, broken only by the frenetic beating of my heart in my ears. The foliage continues a slow creep forward, continuing to wind through the gaps in the trees, choking out the natural underbrush. Panic trickles into my veins. I barely know how I conjured this. How do I stop it?

A figure alights nearby and for a hopeful second, I think it's Draven. But when the figure straightens, I catch lovely curves and a fall of slate gray hair, not the shorn raven locks of my brave, handsome huntsmen.

"You've done enough," the woman says placidly. I turn to look at her and realize it's Ia. "It's time to end it, Princess."

"I can't," I pant. "I don't know how."

My breath is coming too fast. I can't drag in enough air. The weight of the confrontation, the death, Sabre's injuries piles onto my shoulders, bows me forward. A sob breaks through my control and suddenly I'm weeping, the keening cries echoing through the night.

Ia sighs, dahlia-dark eyes examining me with something very like pity. "Princess…"

She crosses over to me slowly, like one might approach a spooked animal. I shy away from her touch. She seems unperturbed, dropping to her knees by my side, sliding a hand up my back. Her fingers slide across the column of my throat, up and up, until she cradles the back of my head with the tenderness of one holding a babe.

Calm slides like cool water across my skin, washing away the pain, the panic, the guilt tying my insides into knots. The nausea fades and fatigue settles over me like a down blanket, swaddling me in assurance.

"Sleep, Princess," Ia commands in a quiet, but firm tone. "It'll be better when you wake."

I have no choice but to believe her. My last conscious exhale shudders out of me. Then my eyes slam shut.

ELEVEN
DRAVEN

"Watch where you're putting that fucking needle, witch!" Sabre hisses, glaring daggers at Ia from his perch on a log.

It has taken him an hour to coax his battered body back to human shape and longer still for Titus to snap all of his bones back into their proper positions. I've never seen him injured so badly. Thrashed by a maple tree, no less. I'd rib him for it if I weren't so damn grateful that he's still alive.

He suffered the injuries for Carmine. He could have made a somewhat clean landing, using his claws on the branches to slow the descent enough to break only one or two bones. He'd tucked her in with his good wing and taken every fucking hit. Carmine had only a smattering of small cuts and bruises to show for the fall, all of which have been remedied with a topical application of liquid ambrosia, helpfully provided by Kassidy's werebear husbands.

Kassidy's husbands.

Gods, that will never stop sounding strange. My ill-bred, foul-mouthed sister, married to not one but *three* royal bears. She's always been focused on her mission, never making time to find love. Fierce and as fucking hardy as a huntsman, I never pegged her as one to settle down with anyone. Perhaps it's fate. Perhaps the sentiment isn't so saccharine after all, and there's truly someone out there for everyone.

Ia tuts. "If you stop moving, it will hurt less. What would your vulgar friend say? Stop being a pussy?"

She jabs the needle into the crook of his arm, pushing the plunger down. More of the liquid ambrosia we'd been given shoots into his veins.

Sabre grits his teeth around another exclamation, letting out a string of muttered swear words instead. It's a day of firsts. My stoic, practical brother taking the route that spared Carmine pain, even knowing it could kill him. Now he's swearing a blue streak, something I've heard him do only once before.

When the village was under attack. When Bacchus stole everything from us.

I'm such a fucking bastard. I'm only tracking Sabre's healing out of the corner of my eye, when I should be at his side. Instead, I'm situated at the edge of the clearing, only about a mile's walk from the Babbling Brook. Wonderland rivers feet into the stream, and the aptly named river can sometimes speak. Carmine's head is nestled into the crook of my shoulder, her soft exhales tickling the skin of my throat every few seconds. Her soft body is molded to mine, legs draped over my thighs.

I need to be focused on my brothers, but all I can concentrate on is the Princess. My lovely, fragile woman.

Not so fragile as I once thought. The grove she'd managed to create in mere minutes had been something to behold. She'd taken out an entire company in minutes. Still, I can't help but shift her closer, hold her tighter.

I could have lost her. Could have found her body broken, limbs bent at odd angles like a chick who left the nest too soon.

I curl my fingers around the underside of her knee. Never again. I won't allow her to be killed. I ought to have been the one carrying her. I ought to have been the one shielding her. I won't make the same mistake again.

Carmine stirs in my arms, curling closer to me, turning her face into my throat. Her lips brush my neck, soft as petals and my cock twitches. I've been uncomfortably hard for a while now, aroused simply my her proximity. In all these years, I've never had cause to touch her like this.

How many nights have I dreamed about tugging her into my arms? Cornering her in some shadowy alcove to kiss her breathless? Hiking her ruffled skirts around those slender hips so I could touch her, taste her, worship her like the queen she is? Wondered how it might feel to be inside her? Would she bite her lip enticingly, arch her back and moan, as I've had women do before?

I haven't had a woman in a decade or more. Not since I was set the task of guarding Leon's daughters. I'd failed Neva, losing track of the Chosen princess shortly after the sack of Ascor. I won't fail Carmine in the same fashion. It's why I've never sought her out in her bedchambers, have never laid a finger on her. Too easy to lose my objectivity. If I know what it's like to be loved by her, I'll never be able to let her go. And she's meant for a prince. She deserves someone her equal.

But Gods, I want to be selfish.

Her eyelids flutter open and the swimming silver, so mesmerizing to watch, fixes on me. Almost at once, they fill with tears. I open my mouth to apologize, perhaps calm her, when she rights herself in my arms.

"Draven!" she gasps, the tears brimming over, spilling down her pale cheeks. They glimmer like diamonds in the morning light. Gods, even weeping, she's beautiful.

Her arms wind around my neck in the next instant and she tugs me down, so there's mere inches between our faces. Then she kisses me.

I'm so stunned, at first I remain still, bewildered. My grip on her slackens, and I'm not quite sure where to put my hands.

Her lips firm and warm, demand a response.

No chaste kisses from this woman. She pulls herself closer, crushing her small but firm breasts against my chest, clumsily trying to arrange her legs around my waist. She winds her fingers into my hair, pulling a little. Warmth shoots into my veins, an answering desire kindling to life inside of me.

It's probably hysteria or a reaction to her near-death experience that's made her react like this. She's just grateful to be alive and whole, and it's come out like this. But I'll take what I can get. If this is all I ever get from my Princess, I'll be beyond grateful.

I can't help myself. I wind an arm around her waist, locking her into place, trying to prolong the experience as long as humanly possible. The other hand comes up to thread into her softly waving hair. It's silken and slides easily between my fingers. I find the roots and tug just enough to give some sensation. Carmine's lips part and a soft, breathy sound escapes her. I press the advantage, sliding my tongue over her bottom lip, tasting her.

She's fucking exquisite, as I've always known she would be. Sweet, like a clover flower and a hint of honey.

Again, she surprises me, her tongue meeting mine in a passionate tangle. She fucking *fights* me, coming up onto her knees so she can hover above me, angling the kiss in her favor. It's a dominance challenge to my beast, but I ignore the impulse to take her to the ground and show her my strength and suitability for mating.

Because holy fuck, I've never been more turned on in my life.

I almost think she'll do more, but the spell is broken when my idiot brother crows aloud. "Fucking *finally!* I thought you two would never get around to it!"

Sabre and Ia are standing beside him.

Carmine pulls away, her lids at half mast, glazed with pleasure and a hint of her earlier fatigue. Her lips are a little swollen, her hair mussed. Even in Titus' overlarge shirt, she looks incredible.

The thought brings me up short, reminding me of my earlier frustration.

Motherfucking Titus. His scent is all over her. Her smallclothes had been near his weapons, the scent of her release potent in the air. I hadn't smelled any hint of his, but even so, I want to castrate him.

Has he fucked her while I slept, knowing I've wanted her all this time? I can't blame Carmine for wanting him. Neither one of my brothers are unattractive and women have always wanted them. It's her choice if she wants to fuck Titus, but I expected him to at least have some fucking loyalty to me and tell her no. Especially as we were camped out in the open.

Titus catches sight of my face and pales, cottoning onto my mood at once. I'll bet the expression is nothing short of murderous. He hastily arranges his own expression into something more serious.

Not fucking good enough. I'm going to beat some fucking manners into him sometime soon. Preferably when Carmine is asleep and Sabre is healed.

Sabre catches sight of my expression as well and seems slightly alarmed. He casts a glance between us, realization dawning on his face. We've been together for decades now, hunting our quarry in a flock when we can. He knows Titus' whoremongering ways, must guess what he's done.

"Perhaps you should take the Princess to the brook, Draven," he says hurriedly. "I'm going to be a horrid patient. Best to spare her ears."

Ia helpfully tugs at the cloth holding his brace in place. The bones will need to be kept straight while the ambrosia does its work. He ought to be fine in an hour or less. He curses loudly, glaring at the witch. She just smirks fiendishly.

Carmine opens her mouth, looks as though she's about to argue that she's not a delicate flower, then closes it again. Some indecipherable thought flits across her face too quickly to be unraveled.

"Yes," she murmurs. "I think I'd like to wash up."

I don't argue, though every fiber of my being demands I set the Princess gently aside so I can take a piece out of my lecherous brother.

Instead, I scoop her up from the ground, using the grip I already have on her waist to cradle her to me bridal style. Carmine lets out a girlish little gasp of surprise, which makes me smile, just a little, despite my foul temper. I don't want to thrash Titus any less, but with her in my arms, I can at least curb the impulse. For now.

I tuck her more securely into me before striding out of the clearing, shooting one last poisonous glare over my shoulder at my brother, a warning to keep his distance until I've gotten a grip. Carmine won't catch it, but the other two sure as fuck will.

Mine, my expression snarls. *She's mine, you bastards. Don't you dare touch her.*

My logical side tells me to step aside and let her fuck Titus if that makes her happy. To sow discord into our band at this point is suicide if we stand any chance at all of killing Bacchus.

But I've never claimed to be logical where Carmine was concerned.

I don't set her down until we've reached the edge of the brook. She stares at me in the oddest fashion, in a mix of that childlike wonder she used to regard me with and... something else. Something achingly vulnerable. I want to cradle her lovely face in my hands again and continue where we left off, kissing the uncertainty away until she smiles again.

She finally drops her gaze to the makeshift tunic she's formed out of Titus' clothing. I hear a distinct sniffle, and it twists at my guts like a well-placed dirk. She's cried so often since joining us. It's my fault. She shouldn't cry over me.

Gods, I'm such a bastard.

I turn away from her so she won't see the warring impulses playing out on my face. Kiss her, take her, plead with her to be mine, and be a fucking selfish animal that values my own happiness over hers. Or continue on as I have, placing her first, even though the taste of her is going to drive me fucking mad at some point.

"You're angry with me," she says.

"No, I'm just... angry."

"Why?"

I shake my head. I can't tell her why. "It's foolish and my own fault, Princess. Don't mind me. I'm not upset with you."

"Carmine."

One of her soft hands comes to rest at the small of my back. I jump and crane my neck to peer down at her. I didn't even hear her approach. She's tucked herself against my side, leaning her head against my arm. The contact makes it harder to think, harder to do what it is I know I must.

"What?" I bark, not meaning to sound so angry but I can't help it. I'm frustrated.

"Call me Carmine. It's so tiresome to hear you all call me Princess all the time. As if I'm ruler of anything any longer."

Her words warm me, tug a smile into something more genuine, not something I slap on for her comfort.

"It's nothing you need to fret about, *Carmine*," I amend quietly.

"Well, if that's true, you ought to have no problem telling me what's troubling you."

I open my mouth, then snap it shut again as I struggle to find an answer. She's backed me into a corner, the clever little minx. She peeks up at me, lips threatening to form a tiny triumphant smile. Those quicksilver eyes dance with mirth.

"I stepped right into that one," I say with a sigh.

"Tell me, Draven. I want to help."

"I need you to... take off that shirt."

Carmine's cheeks unexpectedly flood with color, silver eyes flying wide. I realize too late what my words must sound like and rush to add; "It's the scent, Carmine. I don't like Titus' scent on you."

"*That's* why you're angry?"

I nod. "As I said, it's foolish and it shouldn't bother me but…"

I don't have time to fumble with my explanation. Carmine undoes the belt with sure fingers and, before I have time to protest, she whips the shirt off in a smooth rolling motion. The act bares most of her skin to the cool night air. I think the dress has frayed further, because I can see the full underside of one breast, and the teasing possibility of one of her nipples under the pathetic strip of material.

I should be fucking glad Titus preserved her modesty with the shirt, because I would have been forced to gouge the eyes out of any man who caught a glimpse of her like this. It'd be so easy to half-form my talons and rip away the remaining scraps, leaving her bare.

Take her, take her, take her…

"Better?" she asks breathlessly.

There's still color high in her cheeks. Embarrassment at her almost nudity, probably. I'm a prick. I can't form an intelligent response, all the blood in my brain migrating south. I'm painfully hard now, aching to be inside her.

"Draven, is this better? Is his scent still on me?"

No, it's mostly gone, but I can't focus for an entirely different reason now. "You... you ought to go back to camp," I croak at last.

Hurt flashes across her face. "Why?"

"Because you look incredible, Prin.... Carmine. And I want to do things to you I shouldn't. You go and find Titus now. I won't make you choose between us."

It's the most difficult thing I've ever had to say. To my surprise, she laughs, a short, disbelieving bark of sound.

"Gods.... he was right, wasn't he? You really have no idea."

I don't know what she's talking about and I shake my head. "I know you want him, Carmine. I can scent it when you want a man. It's driven me mad for years. I don't want to make you unhappy, Carmine. If you want him, you should go to him. I won't stop you."

"Draven," she says, exasperation bunching her brow into lines, turning her kissable lips down into a half-scowl. "I can't believe you're such an imbecile."

"Imbecile?" I'm surprised.

"Yes, imbecile," she snaps. "When you watched me, had it ever occurred to you there was one common denominator every time you scented my arousal? The fact that *you* were in the room? Had you ever scented me in my bedchambers, when you came to find me in the mornings? Did it ever occur to you that it was *you* I dreamed about? *You* that I pictured when I touched myself at night?"

My mind churns along slowly, like the first rock tumbling down the side of a mountain, dragging more debris loose until the thoughts slam into me with the crushing obviousness of it. "You want... me?" I ask slowly, sounding out the words. They don't make sense to my befuddled mind.

Carmine stretches up on her tiptoes so she can place her soft little hands on either side of my face. Someone has thankfully had the presence of mind to bandage the poisoned patches.

She sniffles again, more tears spilling down her face, but there's a sweet smile on her lips. "Yes, you idiot. I always have. There's been no one in my heart but you. I can't believe you couldn't see it."

Neither can I. I'm cursing myself for all those hours spent dealing with the frustrating desire alone when I could have had her.

No, you couldn't have had her because she's a princess and you're a huntsman, I tell myself. *It's the same reason I still can't have her.*

She stretches as far as her height will allow, putting her lips only inches from mine. Honey and clover rides out on a breath, fucking intoxicating.

"Do me a favor, please," she whispers against my mouth.

"Anything," I breathe.

She removes one hand from my face so she can rip at what remains of her bodice. It comes away without much effort, fraying to pieces in her hand. It leaves her chest bare. I can't help a small moan when she takes my hand and guides it to her breast. Small perhaps, but soft, pert, and warm. I can't help but draw my thumb across her puckered nipple.

"Make love to me," she murmurs. "Draven, I want to feel you inside me."

TWELVE
CARMINE

The sound Draven makes is caught somewhere between a moan and a growl and vibrates through me like a shiver of pleasure. His lips crush mine, his big, calloused hands securing me to him, one on my waist, another in my hair, just as he had in the clearing.

This time, he doesn't pull away from me. He steps into my embrace, firmly guiding me backward until my bare back hits the smooth trunk of a sycamore. His grip loosens on my waist, sliding instead to my hip, fingers digging into the remnants of my skirts, tearing away the only barrier that keeps me from being completely bare.

Molten desire pools between my legs at the very casual show of Draven's strength. I shudder, and gasp when his fingers quest along my inner thigh. He takes full advantage, stroking his tongue along the seam of my mouth, delving inside when I arch my back and moan aloud. His tongue tangles with mine for the second time in as many minutes, and I can't seem to get my body close enough to his. I cling to his biceps, digging nails into the hard muscles as he rubs warm, teasing circles into my inner thigh, almost but not quite where I need him most.

I'm afraid I'll wake and find this is a dream.

I drag a hand up to his hair, tangling my fingers in the strands at the nape of his neck. I wish his hair were longer, like it used to be, so I could toy with it. But I'll take him however I can.

The kiss becomes harsher, more urgent and I moan. It's so *good*. Better than I imagined a kiss between us could be, all those times I touched myself. Draven is so strong, so tall, his shoulders broad, his body caging mine against the hard tree, giving me no chance to escape.

But Gods, it's all I've ever wanted. So many years of responsibility, of being proper, of being a good girl. I just want someone to strip all of that away. I want to be conquered, utterly dominated by this man.

Draven's fingers finally play along my folds, but he doesn't part them.

He draws back enough to allow me to drag in a ragged breath. His exhale is equally unsteady, warm against my lips.

"Princess?" he ventures, still holding at least some of himself back. Asking permission when I just want him to take.

"Carmine," I correct. "Please, Draven. I want you to say my name, not my title."

He shakes his head and some of the lust in his eyes empties. "I have a duty to you. I shouldn't be doing this. It's…"

"Don't you dare say it's wrong, Draven! It's all I've ever wanted. I *need* you." I take a breath. He can't change his mind now. I won't let him! "Don't stand on ceremony. Right now I'm not a princess and you're not a huntsman."

"I am though," he murmurs, easing just the tip of one finger through the folds of my sex, sliding through my slickness. I'm embarrassingly wet. Wetter than I've ever been, because he's so close. If he would just stop being so damn honorable...

"Am what?" I breathe.

"A huntsman. *Your* huntsman. I failed Neva, but I won't fail you, Carmine. If I fuck you... I'll lose that objectivity. Because all I want to do is hide you someplace where the war can't touch you. I can't lose you. I just... I *can't.* You don't know what you mean to me."

"I do," I whisper. "Because I love you too and I always have."

He goes still, even his breath catches for a moment. His eyes flick down to meet mine, to search my face for the truth.

"You *love* me?"

"Since I was a girl. And I've wanted this for as long as I've been aware it existed, Draven."

"I have wanted you all this time, as well."

I smile. Broadly. "Then could you *please* fuck me?"

"Carmine," he starts, looking confused again.

"No," I insist. "I want to be under you. On top of you. Take me any way you want me. I want marks, Draven. I want to ache in the morning, just so I know this is real, that you've been inside me. I want the world to know I'm yours."

Draven lets out another sound that's a mix of growl and groan. Then he parts my folds and thrusts his fingers inside my channel all the way up to the knuckles. Something inside me pinches, sends a mild flare of pain through me, but I ride out the sensation, moaning as his fingers settle inside of me. I feel so full already, with just his fingers. Will I truly be able to accommodate his manhood? I haven't seen it yet, but I feel it pressing against my thigh. Are all men so large? It doesn't seem possible it'll fit. I'll be walking bow-legged for a while, I fear.

But, I want it.

My nipples pucker to painful peaks as I think of him taking me so hard, I'm boneless, unable to walk. I know he'll carry me. I shouldn't want to be such a liability. But fucking Draven will be worth it.

Draven's free hand finally releases me, tracing along my body in curious exploration, even as his fingers pump in and out of me, firm and demanding, sending a sweet ache pulsing through my channel.

"You want this, Carmine? Are you sure?"

"Gods, yes! Please."

"You want me to touch you? Where?"

"Everywhere. Please..."

His hand comes up to cup one of my breasts, skimming the underside in an almost ticklish fashion. The texture is rough, adding delicious sensation as he pinches the nipple, kneading it to even sharper attention. A mewling sound of pleasure comes from my throat and he chuckles.

He kneads the other to painful attention as well, kissing my jawline, and then presses his teeth into my skin, hard enough I cry out.

Pain. Pleasure.

The snarled mass of sensation in my head sends shocks of confused pleasure through me. Every nip sends want shooting downward, throbbing need making me clench tight around his fingers. His pace stutters for a few seconds and he hisses a curse.

"Fuck, Carmine. You're tight..."

"I want you inside me," I pant. "I need you inside me. Please, Draven."

"Not yet," he says. "I want to taste you."

Almost without warning, he slides his fingers away from my body. I whimper at the loss, tempted to take his hand and guide it back between my thighs again. He brought me close to orgasm, only to leave me hanging. Perhaps I should find it typical at this point. Infuriatingly handsome and oblivious Draven always leaves me hanging.

Then he drives us to the ground, him on top of me, one hand bracing my skull, his descent measured. Moments later, he's settled on top of me. As the warm weight of him presses me down into the mossy softness of the bank, it truly hits me. It's happening. This is finally happening! After years of wishing, secretly pining, it's finally going to happen. I'm bare, spread out before my handsome huntsman like a feast.

He looks as if he wants to devour me whole.

Our eyes meet, and I see the fevered want dancing in their depths. It's the beast, a side of Draven I so rarely have cause to see. Civilized and impeccably mannered, it's easy to forget he's not wholly human. That inside him, there's a creature that prioritizes sleep, food, and fucking over everything else, if it comes down to it.

Draven descends on my breasts with a hungry sound, the warmth of his mouth closing around one hardened nipple. His mouth is incredibly tender and it's almost painful around the sensitive bud. He lavishes it with attention until I'm writhing beneath him. The keen edge of pain-pleasure zings through me, makes my skin feel tight, like I might burst out of it any second. I arch my hips into him when he begins on the neglected breast, giving it lavish attention as well, try to press my wet, aching core against the cock that strains the front of his trousers.

Inside me, I beg silently. *I need you inside me. I can't wait any longer.*

He reads the frustration on my face, sliding one hand down my body to my mound, sliding his fingers into me again. He smiles a little against my skin.

"I'd always wondered," he says, stroking the bud at the apex with his finger.

It draws another mewling sound of pleasure from me. Tears form in my eyes. It's so fucking *good*, so right, so incredible. But, I just want more. I *need* more.

"Wondered what?" I manage to pant.

"Your lovely, little mound. I wondered if it would be bare. I know you don't tend to grow much body hair anywhere else."

"Please, Draven, no more talking."

That elicits a wicked smirk. It's an alien expression on his face, but not one I dislike. It makes him look a little roguish, something I associate more with Titus than Draven. It adds a hint of danger that makes him impossibly more appealing.

He kisses one breast before his mouth trails lower, alternating between nips and feather-light kisses. I jerk every time his teeth graze me, jolts of surprise and pleasure only spurring me on. Gods, at this rate I'm going to be soaked. He doesn't need to do more. I'm more than ready.

He pauses above my mound, inhaling deeply, getting my scent. My cheeks flame, remembering what Titus said. Draven can smell me. Can tell just how he affects me. I have a moment to worry before he groans.

"You're so wet for me, Carmine."

"I want this more than anything."

It's all the encouragement Draven needs. He parts my folds with his fingers, and then his wicked mouth is on me, his tongue stroking along my clit in a move so sensual, it ought to be a crime. I chase the feel of it, trying to keep him right in that spot. His fingers curl inside me, tracing along a spot I can almost never reach with my own fingers. The sweet ache that accompanies the motion tips me over the edge. My back bows, coming completely off the ground, my head rocking back, mouth open in a silent scream of ecstasy.

He doesn't stop. My response only seems to encourage him. Anchoring my hips to the ground again, he keeps ruthlessly on, drawing another climax from me. Then another and another, bringing me to a sobbing orgasm the final time. And even then, he seems reluctant to take his mouth off me. I finally sink to the ground, boneless, my body supple, so completely satisfied, I can't even speak, can barely drag in enough air to moan.

Finally, Draven reaches between us, shoving his trousers down. It's an effort, but I crane my neck to see his erection. I've been so insatiably curious for years now. It only seems fair, now that he's touched me so intimately.

I swallow, my throat a little dry from the screams of pure pleasure he's drawn from me. I admit the sight intimidates me. He's *enormous.* I'm not sure how he'll fit inside me.

"I'm going to fuck you, Carmine," he says, voice rough with desire. My heart lurches toward him, so painfully sharp in my chest.

"Please."

He guides himself to my entrance and then I have to bite my knuckles to hold in more screams. The blunt head stretches me to an almost intolerable level, and then the first few inches of him slide into me. He pushes and stretches me until he's fully seated inside. My body thrums with renewed desire.

He stills above me with a satisfied groan when he's driven himself home.

"So fucking tight," he hisses.

I urge him on, slinging a leg around his waist, pushing myself as close as I can from my position. He rocks his hips into mine gently at first, then with more vigor, thrusting hard against me as I urge him on, whispering filthy things I can't believe I have the audacity to say aloud. I drag my fingers down his back, carving my pleasure into his skin. It actually rips the material of the shirt he wears. He hisses a little and speeds still further, harder, until I spasm around him again.

He lifts my hips, driving himself into me as fully as he can. I climax again, sobbing once more. It's so much. Too much almost.

I love him. I love him and he loves me! And now we're one, closer than I ever dared hope.

Finally, after he's managed to bring me to orgasm again, he stills with a hoarse sound of pleasure. He claims my lips in a fierce kiss even as he spills inside me. Maybe that ought to scare me. But I can't imagine anything I want more than to bear Draven's child. To be his wife, his lover. I crave that sense of normalcy.

But... I will never be normal, will I? I'm more than just an exiled princess. I'm Chosen. I have a destiny and it isn't to be a housewife.

Draven strokes my cheek, wiping away the tears that have spilled down them as we made love.

"I didn't mean to make you cry," he murmurs, lines slashing his brow as he frowns. He shifts almost at once from complacent to concerned.

"I'm crying because I'm happy," I say with a slight hiccup. "That was so..."

Words fail me. There's nothing in the common tongue that can encapsulate what this means to me. What *he* means to me.

Draven smiles, gently disentangling himself from me. He struggles with his shirt for a second before he removes it in a single rolling motion. He offers it to me. I'm too exhausted to put it on at the moment. After a moment of consideration, he folds it and tucks it beneath the pillow instead, before laying down next to me. I snuggle into his chest, pressing myself as close to him as I can manage.

"I know."

My eyes flutter closed of their own accord, fatigue settling over me like a leaden blanket. I didn't know fucking could possibly be so exhausting.

"Sleep, Carmine," he whispers. "I'll be right here, looking over you."

Just like he always has.

THIRTEEN
SABRE

She smells so strongly of Draven when she ambles into camp, I wouldn't be surprised if even mundane humans could scent her. And even if such escaped them, anyone could easily see the trail of purple love bites stretching from the hollow beneath one of her ears, along her neck, and down to the swell of her breasts. She's mostly covered by Draven's shirt, which doesn't allow for more viewing, but I'm willing to bet there's a trail right down to her female bits. The scent suggests he spent a great deal of time using just his mouth before finally taking her.

Her gait isn't so sinuous as it once was. She's not quite limping, but she's moving slowly. I almost grin. Taken hard, then. Not usually Draven's style, so he must have been following a decree from her royal highness to fuck her and do so hard.

Draven is nothing if not accommodating.

I have the briefest image of doing the same. Laying her out beneath me and taking her with enough force she *would* be limping. She's beautiful. Capable. Sure of herself, at least in this respect. All things I like in a woman. The chorus of moans that Titus and I could make out were nothing short of impressive.

Speaking of, Titus is off somewhere, tugging his cock to thoughts of her, no doubt. Better than sporting a massive hard-on for Draven's woman. It would be like waving a flag before a bull.

For myself, I won't get between Draven and the small bits of pleasure he's been able to claim, no matter how beautiful she is.

"Thank you," she murmurs, glancing up at me from behind her thick lashes. Her coyness would strike me as false, if not for her eyes. The quicksilver eyes that reveal her night hag nature are incapable of conveying lies.

I adjust my perch on the boulder somewhat, frowning. I'm mostly healed, but still very stiff. The witch has beaten it into my head that I'm not to shift for at least another day. I don't relish the thought of laying on the hard-packed earth, but I won't monopolize one of the bedrolls when Draven is still weakened. The ambrosia will take care of most of my injuries whilst months or years must have been ground off Draven's life in order to heal his mortal injuries.

I'm just being petulant, at this point. Being earthbound is annoying, but inconsequential in the grand scheme of things.

"For what?" I ask.

"For saving me," she responds. She shuffles from foot to foot, tugs her lip between her teeth and fairly reeks of chagrin. "I'm sorry I didn't say it the moment I woke. You could have died trying to protect me and I didn't even thank you properly. For that, I apologize."

She hesitates and then leans in to brush those soft petal lips across my cheek in a chaste kiss. I have the sudden urge to turn my head, and capture her lips instead. I'll probably taste Draven on them, which will agitate my beast. It's that thought that helps me to simply allow the kiss.

Draven's woman. She's Draven's woman, you selfish old bird.

But it's in a jay's nature to steal. As is the raven's. I wonder if we might be evenly matched if it came to a battle over which of us could give her the most pleasure? I still can't fathom why I want her so badly. Is it some sort of witchery? Part of her allure as a Chosen One? Am I truly so hard-up that I'm willing to cause a rift between my brothers?

A part of me is inclined to take her as a mate, which scares the piss out of me. I do not form attachments for a reason, damn it.

Only Titus' beast doesn't seem inclined to claim her as a mate. It's his purely human inclination to put his cock where it shouldn't be. And that alone drives him.

"I know it's not enough," she says with a wispy laugh. "But I hope that someday I can make it up to you."

I make a noncommittal noise that makes her chew that lip still more firmly. It's damn distracting. If she doesn't stop that soon, I'll be tempted to bite it for her. I can't ask her for what I truly want in this instant. Besides, I think I may be too stiff to manage a rutting to rival what Draven gave her earlier. Perhaps later... no. I can't.

She's Draven's woman, for fuck's sake!

The Princess hesitates before climbing onto the boulder beside me. She swings her legs over the side when seated, mimicking me, directing her gaze toward the forest around us. I doubt she's scanning for threats, as I am.

"Are you still in pain?"

I shrug. "It's nothing I can't handle. I've received worse during the war and the sack of..."

I cut off before I can utter the name. I don't like thinking about Eastmore. The nightmares were bad enough without dwelling on the memories during my waking hours.

"Eastmore?" she finishes.

"I should have known Draven would tell you," I grouse. "He doesn't seem capable of denying you anything."

"He didn't tell me much," she says defensively.

"And what did he tell you?"

She shrugs. "Just that your village was destroyed by Bacchus and you three were the only survivors."

It's still more than I want the average mortal woman to know about my past. It's incredibly demeaning to be pitied, and I avoid it wherever possible. I lapse into silence again, hoping she'll take the hint to leave me alone. She's said her apologies. She ought to go back to Draven.

She doesn't, of course. She's unlike most women I've ever met, in terms of her sexual confidence and willingness to explore, but this? In this instance, she's like almost all the women I've been with. She pecks and pecks at a problem until it either frays to nothing or bursts open at the seams. The tale is ugly and I don't want to tell it.

"I know you don't trust Ia," she says slowly. "But you're following her anyway, just for a chance to kill Bacchus, right?"

"Yes," I say, tone short and clipped. Adding, *Leave it alone, girl,* silently.

She either doesn't hear me or doesn't acknowledge the warning in my voice because she just scoots closer to me. Her warmth is intoxicating and the scent of her release is more potent at this proximity. My beast strains eagerly toward her. She's a fertile, sexually available female. I know what she sounds like when she climaxes. I can make her feel it again.

"Fuck no," I grumble under my breath, batting my impetuous cock down as I have for many years now.

"What?" Carmine asks.

"Nothing." I take in a big breath and sigh it back out again. "It's late, Princess. You ought to go to bed now. We'll be traveling along the Wonderland border tomorrow, and there's no telling what madness we'll encounter there."

It's a clear dismissal, which Carmine, once again, ignores in favor of scooting closer. We're now sitting shoulder to shoulder and conflicting desires do fierce battle in my head.

Pull her closer, so she's half in your lap.

Scent her hair, her swan-like neck, the musky arousal that clings to her skin, even now.

Or push her away, order her in no uncertain terms to return to Draven's side and stay there, where she belongs.

Carmine's fingers play gently along my wrist for a second before she slides her hand into mine, twining our fingers gently. I jerk my gaze away from the surrounding forest to confirm I'm not hallucinating.

No, her soft little hand really *is* twined with mine. She's fucking holding hands with me? After

all she and Draven have done tonight? After she's
still aching from the claiming of her maidenhead?

"I can't," she murmurs.

"Can't what?"

"Can't go," she says, tilting her head up so I
can see the naked, vulnerable concern on her face.
"Not while you look so sad, Sabre. I'm a wicked
girl, but not *that* wicked."

I bark a laugh that startles me. The sound
sputters and comes out in disjointed spurts, like a
spigot left too long unpumped. How long has it
been that I've laughed for anything besides a
cover? I'm skilled at blending, becoming a man
who can charm wicked women. I've never seen
anyone who is *less* wicked than Carmine Resia.

"You're most assuredly *not* a wicked girl."

A muscle in her chin tenses, her lip wobbles
alarmingly. Gods *no*. I will not make her cry.

"I am, though," she mumbles. "I ought to be
happy. Draven is... and we...but..."

"You're not wicked," I insist.

I can't help myself, and I reach out to run my
thumb along her lower lip to still the trembling.
They part invitingly and then the little minx
actually closes her lips around my finger and
delicately licks the tip.

My cock swells, hard almost instantaneously
from just that suggestive little motion.

"I am," she insists, lips moving against my skin in a move that's sensual and distracting. I need to be on watch, damn it. Titus is out tugging his cock to thoughts of her and if she keeps this up, I'll be doing the same before the night is through.

"How do you figure, Princess?"

"Because this really ought to be the happiest night of my life but..." she sucks in a shivering breath. "But I want more."

"More than Draven?"

She nods. "I... it's hard to explain." Then she looks up at me. "I love him, Sabre. It feels like I've loved him my entire life, but I *want* more."

"What more do you want?"

She looks at me imploringly. "I want Titus and... you. How can I possibly be so selfish?"

My stomach lurches when she murmurs the admission. Maybe it should offend me that she's put us on a lower tier than Draven but honestly? There's a small part of me that wants to preen. She wants me.

And Titus, too, which makes me question her taste somewhat. But still.

I say nothing, not trusting my voice. It's apparently the wrong thing to do, because the tears spill over. With a sigh, I wrap an arm around her waist and lift her onto my lap. She lets out a soft little cry of surprise but settles easily enough once I've arranged her so her crimson hair tickles my shoulder and the column of my throat. Her scent swirls around me, potent and distracting. At this rate, I won't scent any oncoming soldiers until it's too late. Scarier still, I can't bring myself to care.

My fingers find their way to her hair, stroking it idly. It's incredibly soft and smells faintly floral. It's very... *her*. I can't find words to describe it precisely, because encapsulating the princess is a feat suited to a more verbose man than I.

She shivers and draws herself closer to me. Does she feel the press of my cock, I wonder? Does it worry her or arouse her more?

"Wanting a thing isn't selfish, Princess. It's what you do with desire that counts."

She's silent for so long, I think she might have drifted off. Her body is soft and pliant against mine, a welcome weight on my lap. Then she turns her head just enough to brush her lips across my throat.

"You're still so somber," she says quietly. "So unhappy. I want to do something to help you. You saved my life. I owe you that."

"Unless you can drag Arcadius before me for gutting, there's not much you can do."

"Arcadius?"

Damn it. What is with my loose, wagging tongue around this woman? I haven't spoken his name aloud in years. None of us speak of that span of days that had made us brothers unless we can help it.

"Who is he?"

I sigh. "A monster." I don't use the word lightly. To some, my brothers and I are monsters, simply for the fact we change shape and live for the hunt.

She seems to be waiting for more, so I elaborate. It seems I'm not going to get the flirtatious woman to sleep unless I tell the tale in full.

"Eastmore tried to stay out of the first war, not unlike the werebears. And we may have gotten away with it if we were a single, unified nation the way they were and are."

"But the Order of Aves has five houses, right?" She asks. "Accipitrine, Corvid, Cathartidae, Strigiform, and Gryphus."

"Draven taught you well."

"The histories taught me well, too," she points out. "Huntsmen have been authorized to kill monarchs before, when they've grown particularly wicked. My Uncle Spyros lived in fear of being assassinated by one of your brethren."

"If my signet ring had sanctioned it, I *would* have killed him. I don't often relish the responsibility, but I take personal exception to familicide. Family is too precious. Anyone who willingly slaughters their own, forfeits the right to their own life."

"Draven said your families were killed. Why?"

"Because the huntsman houses sided with the Guild. It didn't matter that Eastmore was almost entirely filled with untrained women, the elderly, and the sick. It didn't matter that there were only four huntsmen and one huntress in over six hundred living there. Bacchus' revelry swarmed our home anyway, just because they *could.*"

The story has cooled my ardor more effectively than a dip in cold water. Just thoughts of that night. Of Arcadius, pinning my mother's half form to the ground with his hooves, snapping the bones of her semi-formed wings like matchsticks.

She'd secured us in the subbasement with a ward, with only a small sliver of light coming in through a gap between the house and our location. We'd taken turns peering out as the revelry trampled our home and our people into nothing.

"Sabre?"

Carmine's voice jerks me violently back to the present and I become aware of my heaving chest. My grip on her has tightened, crushing her to me like some sort of child's toy, like she can somehow ward off the nightmares.

"Princess?"

"What happened?"

The graphic details would horrify her. They horrify *me,* and I've taken more lives now than I can easily count. The true number will be in a ledger somewhere in House Corvid's record room.

"My mother was assaulted and killed by Arcadius. Anyone who couldn't hide or defend themselves were victimized and ultimately pulped into so much meat under the feet of the revelry. This was all I was able to retrieve of her."

I raise a hand to absently stroke the sleek feather. I've been careful with it all these years, even through the bloodiest of hunts.

The princess takes note of the action and lifts a hand to stroke the length of my braid gently, hovering her soft little hands just above it. I still her questing fingers at once, clenching them tighter than I mean to. She lets out a soft yelp and immediately jerks her body away from mine. She almost topples off my lap and onto the ground. I catch her before she can fall, still faster than she is even while stiff and sore.

"S-sorry!" she mutters. "I didn't mean…"

"Hush, Princess. It's my fault. I overreacted. The shaft contains hydra venom. It's absolutely fucking lethal, even to someone like you. If you broke it, you could kill yourself and everyone else in the clearing."

"But why would you…"

"I have it to use on him, if I ever come face to face with the equine prick again. I want him to die by her hand, in so far as that's possible. I want his death to be painful. I want him to suffer for what he did."

Carmine tries to draw her hand back and, when I refuse to release it completely, smiles softly and places it against my cheek instead. Gods, I need to find a woman. Her fingers are warm and soft and I can't help but press my lips very gently to the bandages on her palm. Much like my mother's last feather, she looks too small and delicate to be as deadly as she is.

Her breath shivers across my face and then she leans in, pressing delicate petal lips to mine. The kiss is short, almost painfully chaste, and perhaps the sweetest anyone has ever given me. I want to drag her back after she pulls away, just to get a fresh taste.

"Why did you kiss me?" I mumble, examining her critically.

The woman's a paradox I don't have the time or patience to solve, but it doesn't stop her from being incredibly intriguing regardless.

"Because you looked so sad," she explains, touching her lips briefly, a small smile ghosting across them. "My father used to say love chases monsters away and that kisses cure ills. I'm not sure I believe it. Still, no harm in trying, though?"

She turns away from me in a sway of narrow though comely hips and begins the short jaunt to the clearing's edge and the river beyond.

"Carmine?" I call after her, for once forgoing the damn courtesy title. Her name feels good on my tongue. *She* feels good in my arms.

She turns to face me with a speculative, half-smile. "Yes?"

"Sweet dreams."

Her hint of a smile blossoms into the real thing, so dazzling and sweet, it knocks the breath from me.

"Sweet dreams, Sabre. See you in the morning."

FOURTEEN
CARMINE

"If they don't shut up soon, I'm going to prune the whole fucking lot of them," Titus seethes, shooting a poisonous glare at the stone wall we're skirting.

The wall is draped so thickly with drecaine vines, it might almost resemble a thick green curtain. The effect is somewhat ruined by the buds that pop along the vines every few feet. White, yellow, and pale pink blossoms chorus swear words as we pass. The vulgar little things seem to be targeting me in particular, and I've managed to learn a few new terms for any and all sex characteristics I possess.

I sigh, adjusting the strap of Sabre's weapons-pack on my shoulder. It's heavier than I expected. He hadn't wanted to give it to me, but then was scolded into submission by both his brothers and Ia. And I, in turn, scolded the other brothers into allowing me to carry my own weight. If I'm to be a Chosen One, the least I can do is learn to carry a damn pack for a few miles.

As to our destination? We are on our way to visit the witch rumored to live in this part of the Wonderland border.

"These fucking things won't stop!" Titus continues, glaring at the plants that continue to spit obscenities at us. Then he unsheathes his sword and looks like he's steps away from making short work of them.

"Don't," I advise, putting a gentle hand on Titus' shoulder. "It's not worth it. You'll be able to tune them out in a few more seconds."

"These little fuckers shouldn't be talking to you like that," Titus responds.

I can't help my smile. It's kind of... sweet that he's defending my honor against the awful, little things.

I feel Titus' gaze on the side of my face, and the heavy stares of his brothers on my back as we continue forward. I keep my eyes fixed firmly ahead, trying to keep my expression as placid and unreadable as the surface of a pond. There's enough to be worried about without parsing out my feelings for the brothers at this point.

Brothers, plural. Gods...

If someone had told me only a week ago that there would be something I wanted more than Draven, I'd have laughed myself silly. How could I possibly want more than Draven? He's... he's everything I've ever dreamed he'd be and more.

And he's continued to be everything I ever wanted. The gimpy pace of our journey has allowed us chances to enjoy each other every night. And we have… with fervor. Often several times in a night, until I'm too boneless from pleasure to move another inch.

But I've managed to kiss both of his brothers during the journey as well. I might have done more with Titus that night, if no guards had found our position. It's a bleak lie to say I haven't thought of the other two in my bed as well. How would they compare to my Draven? Somehow I can't imagine they'd fail to measure up.

Yes, I feel guilty about my musings. Yes, I truly believe I am a wicked girl. But, no, I can't seem to suppress my thoughts or the way I feel.

I've seen the way Titus eyes my breasts. He studies them with the carnal appreciation of a collector who has every intention of trifling with the art. There's a portion of me that wants to strip off Draven's shirt and give Titus an eyeful, just to see what would happen.

Wicked, wicked Carmine.

And Sabre? Well, he's often so implacable, I can't make out what he's feeling. But there's something there. An indecipherable sense of need. I'd caught a little of it that first night I was with Draven. I was finally able to make out the wounded center of a man who did his best to ape a granite statue much of the time. Without that hardened shell, I fear Sabre would break.

Could he let me past his walls? Could he exercise that black fury on my body? Could I even survive his wrath?

The thought has my thighs clenching together with sudden, incredible, and unexpected need. I've been growing steadily wetter as we make our way along, just thinking about the three of them. But the danger Sabre could pose to me makes me paradoxically wet. I know he'll be willing to commit to a level of savagery Draven won't. Something deep inside me wants that. *Needs* it.

Beside me, Titus' steps stutter and I catch the briefest of inhales before he swears.

He turns to glare at me. "Are we going to need to make camp again before we reach Trilby, just so you can fuck Draven?"

My cheeks burn and I dip my chin so my gaze is firmly fixed on my toes. Damn their keen noses. It's damn near impossible to have an idle sexual thought without intrusion.

"That's not..." I catch myself before I can say 'what I was thinking about' out loud. It will beg the obvious follow-up question, which I'm unwilling to answer at the moment. "No. We don't have to stop."

153

I lope forward, hiking the pack further up onto my shoulders, trying to put some distance between myself and the three men.

The closer we get to Wonderland proper, the stranger things surrounding us become. Because this portion of Wonderland butts up against hard reality, our surroundings stay mostly sane, with only brief but startling nods toward the madness that lays just beyond the boundary line. The talking plants and the babbling brook. Gazing pools that don't show reflections, but instead seem to peek into strange locales or reveal something unpleasant about the onlooker.

There are oaks that wind into stairs—stairs that go every direction. And there are giant boulders on either side of us. The boulders are actually enormous books, written in languages I'm unfamiliar with. The books are as hard as rock. Sabre informs me the language of the books is one of six languages spoken in Wonderland. There's also gibberish, gobbledygook, blather, nonsense, and twaddle.

How someone can actually *speak* nonsense, I'll never know.

We're meant to be searching for a door that appears to stand on its own. According to Guild rumor, Hattie's lair is known to shift randomly from one edge of Wonderland to the other. The last they'd heard, it was facing the border with Grimm.

Now? Who knows? It could be as near as a stone'
throw or many, many weeks away.

I don't see why we need Mad Madam Trilby.
We have Ia, don't we? Isn't one crazy witch
enough?

Then again, Ia slips in and out of lucidity. Even
well-fed and well-rested, she tends to speak in
riddles most of the time. I understand why Draven
initially thought she hailed from this barmy place.
She assures us that Trilby is near, but I'm not sure
how much stock I can put into what she says.
Dragons, demons, and shadows, oh my indeed.

I'm so wrapped up in my own chagrin, I don't
keep the keen eye on the ground that Draven
ordered. I stumble over the upraised root of a tree
and smack, head first, into an enchantment.

The spell spasms into the visible spectrum at
once, a violent shade of heliotrope and buzzing
with enough energy to raise every hair on the back
of my neck. Even the skin of my teeth seems to
hum in time with the pulse of magic. It stretches
the length of the clearing, bisecting the wall,
instantly killing the flowers on the vines where it
touches them.

There's a small, head-sized dent in the
enchantment where I impacted and, as I watch, the
magic flakes away from the spot like crumbs off a
well-baked biscuit.

An earth-shaking wail rises from just ahead, like the bass howl of an enormous wolf. The sound sends a spike of pure terror through the back of my skull, punching at any reasoned response I might have. For example, running. For the second time in as many weeks, I freeze in the face of danger. It's Titus who manages to save me this time. He knocks into me just as the enchanted shield balloons outward and forms an enormous hand with fingers the approximate size of oak trunks.

Titus takes us both to the ground, landing on top of me.

Just above our heads, the fingers complete their grasping lunge and flex open when they find nothing. I shudder, imagining what might have happened if I'd remained standing there when the fingers closed. They would have snapped me in half, like the fragile matchstick dolls the chef's girls used to make.

As to Titus and me... Titus' chest heaves against mine, and I have a long, seemingly endless, second to appreciate just how he feels above me. His leg is wedged between my thighs, more accident than intention, I imagine. But still. For just that moment, I'm able to imagine how he'd look if he were pressed inside me.

Then Ia waltzes past our sprawled position, approaching the garish magical barrier with no discernible fear. She tsks at us impatiently as she passes saying; "No time for that now, children. They're coming and they're coming fast."

In the next instant, the wall of magic starts crumbling like the spun sugar glass I've seen in Sweetland. The wall falls to the ground in musical tinkles too cheerful to herald the danger we know is coming.

"I'm sorry," I gasp, trying to push up onto my hands and knees.

My head feels like the bobbin on a spinning wheel, being turned round and around now that I'm upright. I stagger and almost flop onto my back again. Gods, what was that spell made of?

"I'm so sorry," I try again. "I should have known not to..."

"What?" Titus snaps, grasping my bicep in one broad, calloused hand, steadying me before I can hurt myself again. "No one sensed that barrier, Carmine, not even Ia."

"But..."

"No time for assigning blame now. Can you walk, or do I need to carry you?"

I am *not* going to continue this cycle. I refuse to be a weakling they have to tote around like so much extra weight. I will *not* die whimpering on the ground while better men protect me.

So I force my legs beneath me, imagining my back braced with steel, lean hard against the power of illusion I learned from my mother and uncle.

Living in a half-dream is dangerous, because it can distract me, but it's not half as dangerous as staying still in the face of an attack. So I will the dizziness away, imagining I stand as straight and proud as any huntsman. I envision the strength that fled me upon impact is now mine once more.

And it works.

At least, in so much as I can stand without tipping over. The spell is still trying to carom off the inside of my skull, riddling any thoughts more simple than 'run' to tiny pieces.

"I can walk," I grit out.

Then I take a step forward, just to prove it to myself. It takes more effort than I think it should, but with every inch forward, my strength becomes less illusion and more grounded in reality. By the time we've caught up with Ia, Draven, and Sabre, my knees aren't threatening to fold. The inside of my head still rolls every so often, like a lazy wave hitting shore, but at least the turbulent tossing has come to an end.

What I see up ahead threatens to fold my legs all over again.

It's an enormous onyx dragon. It's size is so immense, it's hard to take in at first glance. It's easily the size of one wing of the castle, if not more. I have a feeling if it had a sentient mind, it could have broken off one of the towers and absconded with a damsel. The sight of it, crouched in the clearing just beyond, stirs something in my memory. Not so distant fear, the pang of loss as I saw my phantom sister crouched in the midst of three dragons.

This one looks just as frightening as the beast in my dreams, though with the shadowy veil of dreams ripped away, I can tell it's capable of being wounded. The dragon has one wing flared out to its side, blocking our advance, but there's no wing on the other side to match it, just a strut of bone with tattered flesh hanging down.

But just off to its side are two shapes, one strange and the other frightening.

The first is recognizably humanoid, tall and shapely, and dressed in men's clothing. Heliotrope corkscrews are pressed into submission by a velvet top hat. She has her fingers crooked toward us, more of that bright energy sparking between her fingers. She's sitting astride an enormous tawny lion.

There's something naggingly familiar about her, but I can't examine it too closely while my head spins like a slowing top.

"Calm the fuck down, Hattie!" Titus bellows at the strange lion-rider. "It's just us!"

The woman atop the lion swings her legs over the creature's side and slides to the ground, stalking forward, palpable rage gathering around her, actually seeming to make her corkscrew curls stand up on end like agitated snakes.

"False!" she says, coming to a halt about a foot from where Sabre, Draven, and Ia have taken up their defensive positions. Not one to repeat a mistake, Draven and the rest have made one of the book boulders their blockade to keep most of the dragon fire off them. Only Titus and I are in the open, and my body is mostly shielded by his. It won't stop me from crisping, should the monstrous reptile start flinging fire, but it would keep the worst off for a few moments at least.

I jerk my arm free of Titus' at last, forcing myself to stand straighter. No one is dying on my behalf tonight.

"Truth!" he shouts back. "We're back from a mission with a few tag alongs, that's all."

"You call *her* a tag along?"

Then, to my surprise, Hattie jabs her finger at Ia, not me. I'd assumed, falsely, it seems, that she's angry that I damaged her spell. But her eyes are only for Ia, who straightens to her full height to look Hattie in the face. Draven tries to snatch the hem of her dress to pull her back down, but she sidesteps him easily. I want to shout at her to duck down, but I'm afraid that will draw dragon fire toward Titus, who's still doing his best to shield me.

Ia walks slowly to the middle of the clearing, until she's free of both Draven's position and ours, giving the Wonderland sorceress and dragon alike, the chance to strike her without harming others. She spreads her hands wide, welcoming the blow. She looks incredibly fragile to me in this instant, frozen like the statue of some lost goddess of mercy.

She doesn't *look* like Discordia. Not enough guile in those dahlia-dark eyes, not enough malice in the bearing or the face. The slate hair makes her look older, and a little weary. Only the black dress she still wears gives any hint of the woman she once was. And it doesn't suit her now.

"Your grievance is with me, Hattie," Ia murmurs. "Not them. If you must take vengeance, limit it to your true target. I know how messy your folk tend to be when provoked."

Hattie's eyes narrow on Ia, scan her from the crown of her head to her dirt-caked toes and then...

She blinks.

"Not her."

"What the fuck do you mean it's not her? You said it was her. Who the fuck else could it be?"

A vaguely feminine voice barks the question into every head in the vicinity. It, too, sounds familiar, though, again, I can't put my finger on why.

"Not her," Hattie repeats. "Not her but... not *her,* either."

The feminine voice rustles through my head like the breeze stirring autumn leaves. It's a pleasant, if not a strange, sensation.

"Thanks, Hattie. That's incredibly fucking helpful. Is she here to hurt us or not?"

"No," Ia answers at once. "We're here because the mare and the dragons must needs meet and a djinn's foe aid in bringing Bacchus low."

The lion paws the ground and I swear its great amber eyes narrow on Ia in dislike. The only animal face I've seen emote quite so strongly was my father's.

"Did that make a lick of sense to you, Hattie? Because it means jack shit to me."

"A quest," Ia explains, hopefully better this time. "You and your men are needed to assist another Chosen in facing Bacchus. The new Chosen is Mora. Mare. Dreambane. A night hag."

"Ah, lovely," a new voice says, issuing from somewhere near the edge of the trees.

A man steps out of a hitherto unseen door. And, even though I have had my share of attractive male attention in recent days, I still can't help but stare. He's absurdly beautiful, for a man. A sharp, heavy jaw, a light golden tan that seems to cling to him, though the sun has been a distant thing for weeks now. Fine, golden hair that seems like it was spun so artfully merely to decorate his head, and of course, the eyes. A brilliant tawny, like that of a hawk's, and just as intimidating.

He steps out of the doorway and is followed by another shape. Another man, just as attractive, but paler and a lightly bemused smile. Of the faces I've seen thus far, his seems kindest.

"Just peachy," the golden-haired man drawls. "Because the last time went so well. Salome's attack left the mountains in ruins and forced us to flee. Has her misbegotten spawn come to throw down then?"

It takes a minute for his words to fully penetrate, and when they finally do, the poisonous stew of feelings boils over. These bastards are the ones who killed my mother? Who injured Draven? I'll kill them!

I stalk forward, too fast for even Titus to catch me. He's forced to drop his hand when a prickly briar springs up between us, blocking his restraining hand. Things bloom beneath my feet and spread out behind me at an astonishing rate. I can't seem to stop the gush of power that escapes me, only direct it toward the ground, where it's most useful. At least, until I can get my hands on his arrogant face, that is.

"In fact, she has," I snarl, finally stalking past Ia, putting my body between her and the murderous band before us.

163

I'm not sure if Ia's truly evil, but she's at least done her best to protect me. This man? He's a murderer, plain and simple.

Several pairs of eyes fix on me. I know I don't cut an intimidating figure, drowning in Draven's overlarge shirt, barefoot and filthy and probably reeking of his scent.

No one in the clearing moves. Save one.

The lion's figure dissolves into a thick black mist, hovers for a minute in the air, and then congeals into the form of a tall, shapely woman. She's like a figure cast in chocolate for a few moments, until an invisible hand appears to paint the details onto her body. Alabaster skin, long, pale limbs, and curves I'd have happily sacrifice my right pinkie to obtain. She's completely nude, displaying perfectly proportioned hips and torso. Long ebony hair falls to her waist, but it's her eyes that make me catch my breath.

Edged with thick lashes, the color caught between amber and burnished gold.

"Neva," I whisper.

I release my grip on the power and stagger forward, all my anger dribbling away in light of this newest revelation. I don't know if she's a shade, a revenant, or a fucking mirage. I don't care.

We meet somewhere in the middle of the line, clashing in a tangle of limbs, falling to the ground twined together like Inosculated oaks, never to be parted now that we've found each other again. She peppers my face with kisses, not seeming to mind the traitorous fall of tears that completely contraband my joy.

"Carmine," she whispers, over and over, repeating it like a prayer. And I'm doing it too, repeating her name like an incantation that could keep her here with me forever. "Sister!"

"Neva," I murmur.

The pair of men come to hover over us, wary and confused.

"What's going on?" the golden-haired one asks, eyeing me with faint distrust. "Who's this, Neva?"

My sister pulls away from me and stares down at me with a broad smile. "This is Rose Red," she says, arranging me so I'm mostly sitting on her lap. We're still twined as closely as we can be, under the circumstances. "Princess Carmine Resia. And apparently, a Chosen One."

She grins more broadly then, a bright flash of perfectly straight teeth that no doubt makes her the envy of any woman she comes across. She always was beautiful, Neva. Even as a child.

"Come inside, Carmine, please. There's so much to talk about."

FIFTEEN
CARMINE

The home of Mad Madam Harriet Trilby is a claustrophobic's worst nightmare. There doesn't seem to be a surface in the place that isn't packed with something curious, squirming, or clearly bespelled. It's an assault on the eyes.

The floor is checked, the squares seeming to sway or dance if I stare at them too long. Almost every knob or knocker in the place has faces, with eyes that track me across the room. They're placed in odd, nonsensical places without a door to open at all. I wonder what might happen if I pull them? Would a door magically appear, or would the brass knocker just shout obscenities at me?

There is barely enough space to navigate the hall. I keep bumping into end tables or writing desks, stuffed to bursting with papers and objects I can't name. On one is a complete alchemist's tool set. Something is boiling in one of the beakers, emitting sweet-smelling pink bubbles every few seconds. Hattie bats one away from my face when it comes to bob before me.

"None of that, or we shan't get a sensible word out of you for a week."

"What does it do?" I ask.

"You ask too many questions."

It's actually the first question I've asked her, but no matter. I boggle at the rear-cinch of her waistcoat, which is the only part of her I can currently spy through all the insanity. Then, in the next second, she's gone, leaving me to deal with a floating parasol that does its best to club my right ear as it floats lazily past. I swat at it, then glance upward, prepared for more combative decorations.

Looking up is a mistake.

The ceiling is patterned similarly to the floor, but with red and yellow stripes adorning the dome. They converge at the center, like stripes on a peppermint and form an almost hypnotizing pattern. They also seem to spin when I stare too long. I sway, suddenly dizzy, and I might have collapsed into the next desk, full of miniature cats lounging on satin bows and small, velvety poufs, if Neva wasn't there to catch me.

She gently stops my spinning with a wispy laugh.

"Hattie's home is a lot to take in, Carmine," she starts. "And you don't want to take it all in at once. It'll drive you batty if you try. I'm not even sure you *can* get the full scope of this place. Things seem to change from day to day."

"How do you live here?" I wonder aloud.

Though the more pressing question is how is she here? How is she alive? And if she's been alive all this time? Why hasn't she come to find me before now? It's strange how life works, but I've only known my sister to be alive for the last ten minutes or so and in that time, my mind has been a blank—shock perhaps.

"How… how do you live?" I change the question, facing her earnestly.

Something of my thoughts must show on my face because the good humor drains away quickly, ushering in a more sober expression. It reminds me forcibly of those old days, when Neva's tiny shoulders were hunched over with the weight of the world. The only known Chosen at that point, she'd been kept under almost constant surveillance. Too precious a resource to lose, according to our father. Too precious to be allowed to live an ordinary life. Any semblance of fun had to be scraped and stolen. *A midnight exploration of the dungeon. Afternoons in the arbor. Hiding in alcoves while Draven searched for us.*

I hadn't known what Neva was at that point, nor had my mother. Not until Neva had confided in me, and then I'd confided in my mother.

And then the attacks had happened.

They'd brought in a charred body wearing her shoes. What poor little girl had been charred to death to act as her body double? Did Neva truly resent me so much for my part in what had happened that she'd leave me to live with the guilt all these years?

"I'm sorry, Carmen," she mumbles, reaching out to push a stray curl behind my ear. "I would have come if I'd known."

My steps stutter to a halt, my knees locking, and my hand sweeps up to bat her gentle fingers away from the side of my face. My stomach rolls, a sick sense of betrayal slamming into my gut as solidly as a physical blow.

"If you'd known I was Chosen too?" I hiss, suddenly growing angry as the situation begins to unfold within my mind. "If you'd known there was anything special to return to?"

Furious tears burn at the corners of my eyes, but I refuse to let them fall. I've done enough crying to last me a lifetime.

Neva blinks those huge amber eyes at me once in shock, before an echoing sense of betrayal sweeps over her face. Those eyes go glassy almost at once, tears shuddering on her lashes for just a second before they fall.

"Gods, no! That's not what I meant, Carmine. How can you even think it? I love you."

"You have a funny way of showing it!"

My voice is rising into a shrill shriek, but I can't stop myself. All these years, I've thought I was responsible for Neva's death. All these years, mother never let me forget it was my doing. It's why I've tolerated all of her restrictive rules, all the lectures, all the mind-bending visions she's sent me over the years. Because, somewhere deep down, I knew I deserved them.

I can't believe mother let me suffer all these years, knowing I hadn't killed my sister.

"Carmine," Neva begins, tears falling thick and fast now. A blotchy flush creeps up her neck and into her cheeks. I remember just how hard it is to make her blush. She's as pale as her dearly departed mother, I'm told.

"No!" I shout. "No, Neva! It's not fair! How could you never tell me? I loved you so much and you just…"

My voice falters, cracks and then the lump of unshed tears in my throat becomes too thick to bear and wings the life from my tirade.

Draven, Titus, and Sabre, who've all been perched behind me, move forward, so the line of Draven's body is pressed to my back. His hand closes implacably around my shoulders and he nudges me forward.

"The corridor isn't the place for this conversation, Carmine," he murmurs. "At least get into the sitting room before we crack open this barrel of shit."

I want to argue with him, want to plant my feet and glare at my erstwhile sister until she gives me

the explanation that the situation calls for. But
Draven is right. We can't stay here, clogging up
Madam Trilby's corridor. So I trudge forward,
glaring the point between Neva's shoulder blades
when she turns to troop further inside.

Her skin is infuriatingly smooth and pale, not a
blemish in sight. She's always been incredibly
beautiful. As a child, she looked like a fine-boned
porcelain doll. As an adult woman, she's like a
statue of a goddess, carved from marble. The dress
the blonde man helped her into shows off her
figure to its best advantage. The thing is barely a
slip, made of a silky red material that clings to her
every curve. I know it's probably not meant to
titillate, just something that's easy to slip on and
off for her transformations, but it further pisses me
off. I'll never be as curvy, as striking, as... *perfect*
as my older sister.

The golden-haired man places a gentle hand on
her shoulders when we reach the sitting room.
She's shaking, still crying. He shoots me a dirty
look over her shoulder. I return it with a fierce
glare of my own. I don't care if the damn dragon
despises me for this, Neva owes me an explanation,
damn it.

An army of overstuffed sofas, poufs, and
armchairs crowd around a circular table in the
middle of the room, also done up in the spiral red
and yellow pattern. A favorite of Madam Trilby's,

it seems. Lounging on top of the table is a striped cat, turned upside down so it can support a tea service on its paws. It grins at Harriet when she tsks at it.

"Enough of that, you feather-brained feline," she scolds the thing, rescuing the tea set as the cat rolls to its side. Strangely, none of the cups shift an inch, even as the service tips sideways. Madam Trilby catches me looking and gives me the faintest of smiles, the most friendly expression she's worn to date.

"Sticking charm," she explains. "Cheshire cats are such rascally things. You never know where they'll turn up or what they'll be inclined to smash."

I'm not sure what to say to that and, even if I had a reply handy, I'm not sure I could force it out. My heart thunders like the hoof beats of a hundred charging cavalrymen. My chest feels cold and, if not for the furious tempo of my heart, it might also feel hollow. It's like she's taken a scoop and removed my innards, like one might do to a pumpkin on Samhain.

The blonde dragon shifter sinks onto the overstuffed red sofa and tries to draw Neva onto his lap. I can tell she wants to fold herself into him, but doesn't allow him to do more than draw her into a sitting position. The other two close ranks around her, the black-haired, angry one sitting

beside the blonde, crouching near her like a stone
gargoyle, ready and willing to launch himself at
me. The third one looks just as unhappy, but only
puts a comforting hand on Neva's shoulder and
glances down at her in concern.

"You apologize," the blonde orders. His voice
has been a gentle baritone thus far, but now it's
deepened to something more authoritative.

"Herrick, don't," Neva mumbles. "She has
every right to be angry."

"No, she doesn't," he counters. "It's not your
fault Tenebris put the damn spell on you."

"What spell?" I demand, a little of my anger
fading in light of the new information. It's not gone
entirely, but having some alternative to simply
being left behind is at least more tolerable than
thinking she couldn't be assed to send word.

"N... Neva?" Draven says as he stares at her.

"Draven," she says with a smile.

"I thought... you were dead."

She frowns. "You saw me on the battlefield,
with my dragons."

He shakes his head and frowns. "No."

"Draven, we locked eyes. Don't you
remember?" Neva insists.

He shakes his head more emphatically. "I
can't... I can't remember anything about... the
battle."

"His memory must have been wiped," Neva says. "Before he was taken hostage in the dungeon."

"And the same was done to you," Titus says as he faces Neva. Then he looks at me. "Your father arranged to have the sorceress Tenebris put a spell on Neva after she was safely hidden away, only to be broken by a certain catalyst. The cloaking spell that hid her was tied to it. She was supposed to be shipped elsewhere and we… lost track of her."

I half-turn, slowly craning my head to stare icily at Titus. He flinches away from the accusation in my eyes, dropping his gaze down to the spinning pattern on the floor rather than hold eye contact. Then I look to Draven. "That's true?"

He nods. "It's true."

"You knew the truth about Neva all along?" I ask, the word short and clipped.

There's truly no words for the anger and hurt I feel at the moment. First Neva failed to find me and now Draven has kept this secret from me all this time? After all we'd shared.

"I'm so sorry, Princess…"

"Don't be sorry, give me answers! Damn it all, why does no one *talk* to me? How could you know all this and not tell me? I've lived all this time thinking Neva's death was my fault! Mother brought a charred body to me and told me it was Neva and you let me think…"

Again.

My voice cracks, this time snagging on the sob that's building in my throat.

"I didn't know it *wasn't* her," he says defensively, jerking his gaze back up to mine. "I had no idea Neva was still alive."

There's still a flinching around his eyes. He's truly hurt by my accusation, but I can't stop. I can't. It's like my whole life has been a sham. My mother lied to me, my uncle tried to kill me and now this. The man I've loved for years, whom I've given my body to in the most intimate of ways possible... he didn't even think to mention the *possibility* that Neva was still alive.

Because he didn't know, I remind myself. *He was magicked not to remember the battle. It's not his fault!*

Under any other circumstances, the thoughts might warm me, but not right now. Right now, I'm too angry, too frustrated with the whole lot of them to extend a hand of forgiveness. I want to stroke Draven's cheek, erase the look of abject misery playing out on his face, but I steel myself. I'm through catering to others moods. I'm entitled to have my own feelings about this.

"Sorry about the fire," the dark-haired dragon says sheepishly. "I wasn't aiming for you. Just the night hag."

"The night hag had a name," I snap at him, turning streaming eyes back to the dragons arrayed on the couch. "You could at least say it."

"She was a traitorous hag," he says, standing so suddenly that he upends the books that jut off the end of the table and almost upsets the tea service Hattie has been fussing over. The smell of white tea wafts to my nose. "Your mother sold out all of Ascor to Lycaon and the rest of them. Do you have any idea how many people that killed? And she didn't stop there, either."

"She was still my mother," I insist, swallowing hard.

He continues to glare at me. "Your *sainted* mother came looking for Neva when she discovered Neva was still alive. She stabbed Neva with a drecaine coated dagger. Neva nearly died. She's only just gotten enough strength back to shift. She won't be able to face Hassan for even longer. So no, I won't use the bitch queen's name. *Hag* is suitable."

I snap my mouth shut, cutting off the angry retort I want to lob at him. Because he's right. If what he says is true, I can't fault him for hating my mother. But she was *my* mother. I may not have many pleasant memories of her but... she gave me life. She raised me, taught me as best she could. And, now that I think about it, she tried to protect me, in her own way. She had to have suspected I was Chosen when the poisoned patches sprouted on my palms and yet, she hadn't killed me or sold me to someone who would.

"I think there's enough to worry about without assigning blame, Malvolo," Neva says, leaning her weight back against Herrick's chest. "The point is, we're all here. We're all safe, and there's plenty of time to divulge what's happened in the last fifteen years."

I settle unwillingly onto a scarlet pouf and rest my head in my hands. I shy away from Draven's touch when he tries to take my hand, instead inching closer to Titus, who's come to sit on my other side. Draven lets his hand drop after a second, and it clenches into a fist on his thigh. His devastatingly handsome face smooths into something unreadable. A pang of guilt twists just below my navel, but I shove it away.

Madam Trilby pours us all a generous measure of tea, and I take long pulls of mine, savoring the scalding slide down my throat. It thaws some of the cold that rests on my chest and settles the nausea that's threatened since I impacted Madam Trilby's warding spell.

And for the next hour and a half, I'm regaled with tales of Neva's past, both as a dancer at the Wicked Lyre tavern in Ascor and her more recent adventures with her three dragon mates, Herrick, Malvolo and Reve.

She glosses over the former, an almost haunted look in her eyes at what she has to recall. Gooseflesh springs into being on my arms and I feel like the worst sort of scum for making her relive this, for being angry with her in the first place.

She seems grateful when Herrick shifts the topic to the exploits of Neva's friend Kassidy, the guild thief, and what she knows of the woman's journey to retrieve Sorren's heart. Ia is able to jump in to finish the tale, a sour twist to her mouth as she recounts what Discordia said and did in the moments leading up to her defeat and subsequent power drain.

"So there are three Chosen that have already emerged," I say, a hint of wonder in my tone.

Sabre's been oddly quiet since we've arrived, observing me in silence. Titus has curled me beneath one arm, holding me fast to his side at my insistence. He keeps sneaking glances at Draven over my head, but it doesn't stop him from lightly petting one of my thighs. I try not to focus too intently on it, lest I get excited. It's bad enough the three of them know any time I'm aroused. At least they all know my arousal is strictly for them. The mortification of having Neva's men know that I'm stimulated... well, that might be too much to live through.

"Four?" I repeat, casting Sabre a curious glance.

He nods. "Kassidy encountered the exiled Princess Arianwen during her mission in Delorood. Aria staged a coup against Triton with Kassidy's help and came into her power in the process. She sent Lar, Sol's twin and loyal lieutenant, scurrying to find dry land. I hear she's formidable."

I can't help another twist of anxiety. So many formidable women. I don't think I can count myself among them. I've been nothing but a burden to my daring huntsmen, have done nothing of note except to kill my own country's men at arms. I couldn't even defend myself against Madam Trilby's spell. Titus had to save me.

Some Chosen I am.

"I think we ought to get to bed," I mumble, casting a longing glance toward a darkened hallway near the back of the room. "I've had enough surprises for one day."

I need a soft bed and the space to let the melancholy show. Somehow, even knowing Neva is alive, I can't dig up the proper enthusiasm. Every new development shows me I'm unworthy of the power I've been granted. What was Zephyr thinking when he bestowed Morningstar's blood on me? I'm nothing special. Not brave, or strong, or smart, or even particularly kind. But what I am is exhausted—mentally and emotionally.

"Agreed," Neva says with a yawn.

She stretches, and it lifts the silken material of her slip an inch, exposing more creamy thighs. Three sets of eyes fix on the bared flesh and their hunger is palpable. Something tells me Neva won't be getting as much rest as she'll need for the journey.

Madam Trilby says the quickest route to the Anoka mountains lies through Wonderland. We'll be wading into the thick of the mad world. That means we'll need to be on our guard, especially as the Queen of Heart's guard patrols the border. Rumor has it that the Knave of Hearts has been exiled, and the Queen's Valet now leads the troops. She's rumored to be a fearsome, golden-haired warrior whose temper is only matched by her cruelty.

Whatever the case, we'll have to be on our toes.

I ignore Draven's hand when he offers it.

"Carmine," he whispers, tone pleading. "Please."

"In the morning," I say, curling into Titus' side, sliding my hand into his instead. "I'll speak with you in the morning, Draven, but not before. Let me have tonight."

The hand drops to his side once more and he nods. "Fair enough."

They're not the words I want to hear. Paradoxically, I want him to fight me. Insist on accompanying me to my bedchamber, fuck me so hard and thoroughly, I can't remember my own name.

But I say none of it aloud, instead allowing Titus to lead me to the last door on the right. The door is paneled oak and carved in what I think is gobbledygook or maybe it's gibberish. It's all nonsense anyway.

Draven pads down the hall and disappears into a room very near Neva's. I stare after him for a long second before the door slams closed behind him. I wince.

"You ought to be kinder to him, you know," Titus says, following my gaze. "He truly does love you. More than anything. He'd cut off his right wing if you asked him to."

"I just… it's been a long day and I can't think any longer," I start, even realizing Titus' words are true.

"I think he wants you for a mate."

I jerk my head up at him. "A mate?"

He nods. "You ought to ask him. Might be nice to have a life partner before we all die in the Anoka Mountains."

"We won't die," I promise him as much as myself.

"I hope not, Princess," he says with a chuckle.

"Thank you for telling me… what you did. About Draven."

He nods. "You're welcome."

And then we just stand there, neither of us making a move to leave each other's company. I swallow hard as I wonder why and then, a second later, realize why.

"What do you want, Titus?" I murmur, and I can't help but step closer. I wind my hands into the material of his shirt, pulling him closer. He sucks in a surprised breath and presses himself closer to my body.

"Carmine…"

"Why haven't you left for your room, Titus?"

"Because I don't want to," he answers.

"Why?"

"Because I want to fuck you," he admits. "To know what you feel like, gripping my cock. To taste your pussy and worship those perky little breasts." He says the words with fire in his eyes, but seconds later, he steps away. "But it's selfish of me. You're Draven's."

"Maybe… maybe I don't have to be his alone," I point out. "Neva's men share her. Kassidy's husbands share her…"

"Birds aren't dragons or bears, Princess. We mate for life."

"But maybe all three of you… could?"

He chuckles and bops the end of my nose with the tip of his index finger, like I'm his child sister. "I don't know if you could handle even two of us."

I stand on tiptoe, so our faces are only inches apart and offer him my mouth. He doesn't seem to be able to help himself. He backs me into the paneled door, hands coming to rest on my waist as he slants his mouth over mine. Just like before, his kiss makes me dizzy with want, desire coiling low in my belly.

It's a long time before he releases me and retires to his own room. It takes even longer for my heart to stop throwing itself at my ribs.

I trace my swollen lips idly.

The kiss was wrong, will probably upset Draven. But in this moment, I'm thinking of Titus, of the hardness he pressed against me and how good it might feel to have him inside me. And then I begin thinking of Sabre and I think of Draven too. I think of them… all three together, inside me.

I'm truly a wicked, wicked girl.

SIXTEEN
TITUS

Wonderland is giving me a fucking headache.

While there's no denying it's beautiful, it's also incredibly garish in places. Gaudy colors slathered onto flora and fauna of improbable size, all of them bunched so tightly together, there's a sense of claustrophobia, even in the open.

Even the stone path we're walking isn't mundane. The cobblestone is a rich lapis lazuli, occasionally dotted with what looks like sapphires. In any other place, the gemstones would be precious, but not here. It shouldn't surprise me the Wonderland folk value oddities and trample wealth beneath their feet.

This backwoods path is supposed to be taking us through one of the less-traveled portions of Wonderland, where the guards don't often travel. It's been claimed by the Church of the Seven Joys, the strange new religion that's cropping up all over Fantasia, despite the fact most people tend to avoid Wonderland folk when they can. Hattie says Seven Joys believers don't often resort to violence, so it's likely safe to travel here. The worst they're likely to do is proselytize in our general direction, and there are no easy converts among us.

The Princess walks stiff-backed ahead of me, standing shoulder to shoulder with Draven. They need to have a discussion sometime soon, because the atmosphere around them is becoming oppressive. At the very least, they ought to fuck, if only to relieve the tension.

I adjust myself discreetly. I've been more distracted than I care to admit with Carmine around. No longer in Draven's shirt, she's wearing one of the silk slips that Neva wears, though Carmine's is black, not scarlet. It contrasts strikingly with her crimson hair, and I can't help but watch the sway of her curls against the fabric, can't help but admire how it hugs her cute little ass, and shows off what cleavage she has.

I've been fantasizing about tasting her breasts since she asked me the question in the corridor. Why wouldn't I retire to my bedroom? Why did I linger there, with her?

I want to taste her so badly, it's beginning to hurt. I mulled over her words all night.

I don't have to be his alone. Neva's men share her. Kassidy's husbands share her too...

Sharing.

I'm not sure it's something the three of us are capable of. Sabre's so picky about his women, I imagine he'll guard the one he finally picks jealously. Draven's had his heart set on Carmine for years. And me? I'm not sure I'm capable of loving at all, nor committing to fucking one woman, no matter how incredible the sex may be.

I have no doubt sex will be phenomenal with the princess. Judging from the sounds we've heard from her matings with Draven, she's sure to be a spirited bedmate. But can we truly share one woman? I know the dragons have done so before, all of them centering a relationship around the huntress Peregrine, but I've never heard of a huntsman doing it.

I try to picture it. Draven fucking her mouth while I slide into her warm, slick pussy. The sounds she'd make, the way she'd look, eyes glazed with pleasure, her nipples hard enough to score glass. My cock grows harder. Damn it. At this rate it's going to be impossible to hide just how much thoughts of her arouse me. Worse, Draven might scent it. He's rearing for a fight, and this isn't the time or place for a brawl. If he wants to vent his aggression, he should do it on her pretty pink pussy, not on my face.

We come to a fork in the road, at the crux of which is a sign. It points in every direction. *This way, that way, near, far, wrong way, dead end,* and *do not proceed,* are only a few of the many arrows that direct the unwary traveler. I'm sure they mean something to a Wonderland native, but to me, they look like unadulterated madness. What fool takes a path that reads 'wrong way'?

Us, apparently, because Hattie immediately turns onto the path leading that direction.

The path is gloomy, shaded by enormous, rather fragrant gilled mushrooms that arch over the path. The scent is earthy, with a hint of something less benign. At least a few of these mushrooms are poisonous.

My vision is less acute in the dark than I'd like. Damn my mixed breeding. Why couldn't my grandfather have fucked a Strigiform huntress instead? Sabre and Draven are little better off. It keeps us all on edge, eyeing each shadow with suspicion, as though something might spring from them at any second.

Hattie and Ia lead the procession, as they're arguably the most potent magical defense we have. Neva and Carmine trail behind them, flanked on either side by the enormous dragon Generals. While Carmine and Neva are destined for greatness on the battlefield, they're still young. Untried and untrained, which means they have to be protected until such time as they're ready to face down Morningstar.

And then there's the three of us, bringing up the rear, ready to take on an assault from behind. It's a good defense posture.

So why do I feel so antsy?

Something about this place sets my teeth on edge, rings every alarm bell in my head, telling me to take Carmine and find a different path. I don't think it's merely the lack of visibility, though that certainly doesn't help. It's.... something malevolent. Something more than the charged air of chaotic possibility that hangs in the very air of Wonderland.

A glance to my right shows I'm not alone in my concern. Draven has a grip on the dirk sheathed at his waist. He scans our surroundings every few seconds, keeping a keen eye on the shadowy spaces between the pale gray mushroom stems. Sabre's thumbing the hilt of his sword, stroking the tightly braided pattern that adorns the spot just beneath the hand guard like it's a beloved pet.

A glance to my front shows the dragons are similarly on edge, though they're hiding it marginally better for the sake of the women between them. Their muscles tense beneath their tunics, hands forming into claws at their sides, necks craning to find the danger.

Only Neva and Carmine seem undisturbed, chatting away happily. Now that the misunderstanding has been smoothed over, they seem to be mending their broken relationship, recounting what's happened in the last several years. Neva is rather tight lipped, except to say that her former master, Darius, was less than kind to her. Carmine doesn't press for more details.

I suspect she doesn't want to know.

Eventually, we come to the end of the mushroom row, stepping into bright sunlight at last. It's not much, just a few patches were the light dapples the ground. I'm so grateful for the illumination, I could kiss the cobblestones. At last I can fucking see more than a few feet in front of my face.

I catch a glimpse of Carmine up ahead, stepping into one of the patches of light and for a moment it knocks the breath out of me. Framed by the soft squares of light, she looks like a fucking goddess. Her crimson hair is loose around her slim shoulders and shines with bright highlights. Her ivory skin practically glows, and the black shift does little to hide her silhouette.

In that instant, I want to kiss her more than anything. Tug her tightly to my chest and plunder her mouth until she's breathless for me. Slip one strap of the shift off her shoulder and taste that luminous skin.

I grind my teeth, catching myself before I can descend into pointless daydreams. It's not the time for this and she's not mine. Nothing's been decided yet. There's been no conversation with Draven.

She tilts her head curiously, examining something. I follow her gaze. Just up ahead, in the shade of more mushrooms, is a large building. It's curiously shaped, like someone constructed it incorrectly. The base looks ordinary enough, composed of the same stone as the road. But about halfway up, the building bulges outward, dwarfing the base like a too-large book piled atop its smaller fellows. The top of the building is wider still, giving the impression that the thing has been tipped over and rests on its head now, instead of a base.

Atop the building, is a cone that ends in a large sun symbol. It looks familiar, somehow, though I can't place my finger on just why.

There's what appears to be a garden just off to the side, and tending it is a man in the purple robes of a priest. He straightens up as he hears our approach. He's young, perhaps in his mid-to-late twenties, with white-blonde hair and wide, dark eyes. In the dim light available, they almost appear black. Around his neck, he wears a smaller version of the symbol, this time done up in steel.

Unease trickles through my veins at the sight of it. And him. What is the symbol? Why are my senses telling me to draw my scythe? It's not the pendant itself. The thing is sharp-edged, but it's unlikely to be able to do much but act like a shuriken in a pinch. Not enough to kill most of our group and the ones fragile enough for that are nestled in the middle, away from harm.

The man's face breaks into an almost boyish smile of delight as he catches sight of us.

"Welcome friends!" he says jovially. "What brings you to my doorstep? Would you perhaps be interested in hearing the word of our saviors?"

"No, thank you," Malvolo bites out before the rest of us can speak. I can tell the General is trying to be polite, but failing.

The priest is undeterred. He steps out from the row of colorful blossoms, ignoring the longing sighs of the pink lady slipper blossoms as he passes. He sets the watering can down on the ground and makes his way toward us, arms extended like he might snatch Hattie up in a hug. There's something strange playing out on Ia's face, like she's choking on a lemon wedge and can't clear it from her throat. Hattie just watches him approach with mild disdain.

The man is much shorter than most of our party, only breaking even in height with Carmine, who is, without a doubt, the smallest among us. That still puts him at around five-foot-six. His hands are calloused, used to hard labor, but they're empty of a weapon. They're not even curled into fists.

So what is wrong with this picture?

He smiles and bows at the waist, inclining himself respectfully in Hattie's direction and, I suppose, Ia's as well. Ia still looks like she's going to choke on her own tongue. I feel an unwilling trickle of concern for the witch.

"Madam Trilby, I'm Brother Claude Frollo. The table is set and a hare's feast prepared. Share our table, we who oppose the bloody big head with you."

The words fountaining out of his mouth make no goddamn sense to me, but they must mean something to Hattie because she nods.

"I'll take tea. My friends need take no part."

Something flickers through Frollo's black eyes for a moment, and his lips purse almost infinitesimally. I finally give up the battle against my reasoned mind and slip my hand into the coat Harriet provided me, rummaging through the many oversized and seemingly bottomless pockets to find my chain scythe. I end up producing a shower of buttons, a small mouse, and a few quills before I find the pocket containing my weapons.

I draw the chain scythe as quietly as I can, cursing the small clinks and rattles as it comes loose. If Frollo notices, he doesn't acknowledge it.

"All or none, I'm afraid. It is my gods' way. They will you all to sit at their table."

Hattie glances from the church once, around to the rest of us and sighs.

"Would it be a terrible inconvenience?"

"I don't think we should," Ia croaks.

Hattie whirls on her, the move so quick and graceful, it's almost a pirouette. Her patchwork coat flares wide and her almost inhumanly wide eyes narrow on Ia.

"You are a thorn in my side at every turn."

Ia doesn't flinch away from the Madam's advance as I would. No matter how fucking brave a man is, there's a limit to what he will and won't do. I, for one, don't like fighting women at the best of times. Feminine thinking eludes me on my own side of the divide. I don't want to see what batshit logic a Wonderland woman can come up with.

"I was once perfect harmony. Of course you dislike me. But at one point we did dance together. Do you recall?" Ia asks.

Hattie blows out a frustrated breath. It ruffles Ia's hair, but she doesn't back down.

"Why should we not enter the good man's home?"

"I..." Words fail Ia for a moment. She frowns, tries to regroup, but can't conjure the proper response.

"We lose only ten minutes," Hattie argues. "What can happen?"

"A great deal," Ia murmurs. "A great deal, my dear Hattie. But we'll do this your way."

And just like that, the decision is made, our guide making the call for all of us, without even so much as a consult. I tuck my chain scythe back into

my coat pocket and take up a position near
Carmine as we troop toward the misshapen church.

Ia may trust Hattie's judgement, but I'm not
sure I do. No matter how well-intentioned, how
seemingly kind, Hattie is mad. Everyone is mad
here. Wild and unpredictable.

I stay close to Carmine, ready and willing to
shield her from the madness to come.

SEVENTEEN
CARMINE

The interior of the church seems larger than the outside would suggest. It's dim, shaded in hues of violet and black, giving me only the vaguest impression of pews that crowd the center aisle. The windows of the church appear to be shielded by large metal shutters. They block out almost all light, leaving the only illumination at the front of the room.

There's a feast laid out at the front of the room, a long table easily able to seat twelve situated on the dais. The light appears to be filtering in from above, glancing off spinning metal sigils suspended from the ceiling.

The imagery of the sigils is interesting: a full sun, beaming out light and heat. A pair of intertwined dancers spinning with glasses in their free hands. A sword wrapped by vines. A flaming wolf's head. A sparking wand and golden crown. An oil lamp and a single, dazzling star. It's the star that burns the brightest and sheds the most light.

They all seem... oddly familiar, somehow, but I can't quite recall when or how I've seen them.

I'm so fixated on the symbols, I don't immediately notice that the blond dragon in front of me (Herrick, I believe Neva calls him) has stopped in his tracks. Neva knocks into me on the other side and lets out a little yelp when she runs smack into the back of General Malvolo, who's also gone still. They're so tall, I can't really make out what's going on ahead, and can only catch glimpses from between their elbows.

"Herrick? Mal?" Neva asks, rubbing her smarting nose. She looks a little agitated.

Me? I'm a little frightened. There's a sort of... oppressive atmosphere in the church I don't like.

Titus steps closer to me on the other side, drawing his chain scythe out from his coat almost soundlessly, ready to extend the chain and let it fly at a moment's notice. Draven and Sabre come up behind us, pausing as well, so that Neva and I are caged in by a wall of tensed, capable muscle. It should make me feel safe, but at the moment, I feel trapped.

"Fuck," Reve breathes, at the far edge of the line of dragons. What I can see of his face has gone ashy pale. "Maenads."

A shiver of pure panic dances down my spine at the word. *Maenads.* Zealous followers of Bacchus and the creatures that made up a good portion of his revelry.

I peer around Herrick's elbow as best I can, so I can get a glimpse of them. When we first walked into the room, no one was sitting at the table but now it's surrounded. There are nine total, discounting the priest, who stands meekly by with his head bowed in deference toward the table's occupants. The occupants seem to be divided into two groups and they're as disparate in appearance as can be possible.

The maenads seem to have skin the color of cream and tawny locks that tumble around their shoulders. They wear wreaths of ivy around their heads and each seems to be carrying long staves wrapped in ivy. Many of them are wearing fawn skins, though a few are completely bare, slender and perfect, compelling despite the terror their presence invokes. These few are only wearing gently undulating snakes around their throats, like living, deadly scarves.

The other half of the table's occupants is made up of equally terrifying figures, though these are darker, more wraith-like than the maenads who, for all their frightful power, still look relatively human. These... do not. They range in size, shape, and color, but none of them could pass for human. There's the skeletally thin female figure that hides most of her face beneath a cowl. It's the hands, feet, and wings that peek out from under the fabric that give her away. The skin stretched thin over bone is mottled gray, the feet, such as they are, cloven, and the wings membranous like a bat's.

The figure next to the woman is impossible to identify as male or female. It has a human torso, yes, but so lumpy and shapeless as to be no help in identifying a gender. The head seems to lay atop the shoulders, with almost no neck to speak of. The oblong circle has a beak instead of a nose, no ears, and clusters of eight black eyes placed on either side of the beak. They blink eerily at us as I watch. The waist tapers off into a thorax and then, to my horror, eight hairy spider legs.

A pair of doll-like girls perch on top of the table, passing a haunch of beef between them, tearing massive hunks away with rows of needle teeth. Every part of them looks stitched together from different parts. I can spy siren, dragon, bear, and bird, even at this distance. They're joined at the tail, so it almost seems to form a long rope between the pair.

And then a man steps out from the shadows to join the fae, making the number at the table an even ten. He looks almost mundane after the eerie visages of the maenads and Unseelie fae (because I have no doubt Unseelie fae is what they must be).

There's no denying he's pretty, in a roguish sort of way. I like that quality in men, which is why he outshines the priest in my estimation, even though Claude Frollo is nothing to sneeze at.

This man is built along the same lines as Titus. Broad-shouldered and muscular, though he somehow looks more proportional than Titus. He's taller by at least a foot, putting him closer to Malvolo's height than any of my huntsmen. He's dressed well too, in a rose-colored overcoat that seems unusually bright in the room. He wears dark trousers and there's the visible bulge of a sword peeking out at around waist-level. There's at least two more blades tucked into his bootstraps.

His hair is closer to umber than chestnut, and tied in a tail at the back of his neck. It almost obscures the vivid scarlet streaks in his hair. His eyes are a lovely cinnamon color, his jaw strong and square, his nose long and straight.

A tremor runs through Titus and I place a gentle hand on his elbow on reflex. He flinches, glances down at me with anguish in his eyes, and then returns his gaze to the figure on the raised dais.

"Gatz," he says in a low voice, choked with pain.

Gatz.

I recall that name dimly from the night when we spoke. Gatz is Titus' cousin. A Gryphus Huntsman who was or is in love with Belle Tenebris. The one who turned traitor. And now he's here, with Bacchus' people, ready to kill us. Just like Titus feared.

I tighten my grip on his arm, trying to assure him of... what I don't know. I can't make this easier on him, but I want him to know I'm here for him, all the same. That some, small part of me loves him. Loves all of them in a way.

Gatz's eyes flicker to Titus' face and then scrunch in an echo of Titus' pain. Those eyes do truly seem sorrowful, even as Gatz draws his longsword.

"Cousin," he says, inclining his head toward Titus. "I had hoped the rumors were false. I hoped things wouldn't come to this."

"They don't have to," Titus says, gingerly removing my hand from his elbow. With his hip, he edges me back and into the waiting arms of Sabre, whose arm winds around me at once, the other producing a crossbow from the interminable interior of one of Hattie's coats. Sabre has to aim carefully, lest he hit one of Neva's dragons.

The dragons can't move, or they'll expose Neva. We're trapped in a tight knot, with the frontline unarmed, Neva and I in the middle and unable to exercise our powers safely, and the rear guard unable to move as well.

The sorrowful lines around Gatz's mouth and eyes deepen, even as a forlorn smile twists his full mouth.

"Titus, you know that's not true. This was always the way it was going to play out."

"For fuck's sake, Gatz! You know Tenebris is on our side! Why the fuck are you climbing into bed with these fuckers?" Titus insists. "You defeat the Guild and then, what? How do you expect Belle to forgive you if you slaughter everyone she's committed her life to protecting?"

A muscle in Gatz's jaw ticks and some of the sadness gives way to frustration.

"She'll see things my way eventually. She'll be my mate and we'll be happy together. Morningstar promised that if I slay even one of the Chosen, I can guarantee Belle's safety. She'll be mine. She'll bear my children. Morningstar has promised."

"You don't want a wife," Titus counters. "You want a whore. Gather up some gold and find yourself a bevvy of whores if you want a beautiful woman who'll lie to you."

"I want Belle," Gatz insists.

"Don't you dare fucking claim you love Belle if you're throwing in with them."

All geniality drains out of Gatz's face at last and he raises the sword. Then Gatz moves, faster even than what I've seen from my huntsmen. He's off the dais in a half-second and thrusts the blade at Malvolo in the next, barely missing his heart.

The General is quick too, twisting to the side to avoid Gatz's attack, leaving an opening to get to us. Exactly what Gatz planned.

A little shriek spills from my lips as the blade sails past Malvolo's shoulder and straight into Neva. Only... Neva's body dissolves into something oozing and black, barely resembling her human shape. It bubbles and writhes and, as I watch, begins to devour the sword inch by inch until the blade completely disappears into the frothing blackness.

Gatz is forced to let go of the hilt before the blackness can touch his fingers. He staggers back, watching with horrified fascination as the golden hilt disappears as well.

Herrick throws a punch into Gatz's side, which lands a glancing blow before the huntsman can backpedal toward his allies. Gatz has a weapon in his hand before I have time to blink, a small sun-shaped disc, not unlike the one the priest wears. He's loosed it in the next instant, and it sails for me. I don't even have time to scream as the thing hurtles toward me.

Sabre whips me out of the way, in a move so sudden and violent, it wrenches my neck. In a furious few seconds of movement, Sabre moves us to the back of the room, near the doors. He scrambles to find the knob and curses when he finds only flat wood.

One of the naked maenads lets out a trilling laugh before casually rounding the table. There's something mesmerizing about the way her hips and breasts move as she walks, and the way the snake trails its way down her body.

"Wonderland is simply marvelous, is it not? Reality bends at a whim. It's why we set up the churches here first."

Only then does it click.

The Church of the Seven Joys, the religion everyone has brushed off because it comes from Wonderland, allowing it to unobtrusively steal across Fantasia. Morningstar's seven generals, with Morningstar the penultimate god to reign over all. How in the name of Avernus had we missed it?

"You can't get out," she continues with a sly smirk. "Hand the Chosen Ones over and the rest of you may be spared. Our Lord is merciful. Thilde can remove their souls from their bodies. It's almost painless."

In answer, Reve actually lifts the front pew and swings it at her in a move so fast, it's hard to track. He bats her away like all of this is a child's game of ball. The maenad smacks into the wall with a crunch.

"Herrick, shift!" he shouts at the blonde dragon. "We'll shatter the place if we have to."

Herrick nods, not even bothering to shed his clothing before he begins. His shoulders hunch and bones slide and snap into new positions. His spine elongates, the vertebra standing out starkly against the skin. More of them crowd into place as I watch.

The golden cast to his skin becomes a truly metallic shine and a scale pattern etches itself onto it.

Within the span of a few seconds, Herrick has grown immense in size, his bulk ever increasing, crowding the rest of us into corners. When a tail whips into our corner, Sabre grabs onto a spiny protrusion and uses it to guide us onto Herrick's back. He has me tucked into his body, protecting me as Herrick's great, scaly head rams the ceiling, wood splintering and raining down on all of us.

A warm spurt of scarlet drips from Sabre's cheek, droplets pelting my face as we rise up and up and up. My eyes burn. He's suffering injury for me. Again.

Herrick's wings can't quite clear the building, but it doesn't truly matter. The instant the opening has been cleared, Neva is in motion, her amorphous form solidifying into a rather large battering ram that slams into what remains of the ceiling. Again and again, she rains down blows until Herrick is able to get first one and then the other wing free.

Shrieks from below alert me to the battle raging on the ground. The maenads and Unseelie fae haven't remained idle. They're climbing up Herrick's back, tearing at his scales in an effort to get leverage. Some of the maenads rip his scales in their mad dash upward, and Herrick's body twitches spasmodically. He flicks his tail hard, in an effort to send them all flying, but only manages to unseat one of the clothed maenads. The nude ones almost seem to have fused their skin to his scales and crawl up on their bellies toward us, smiles on their faces and madness dancing in their eyes.

Worse, the effort it takes for Herrick to buck them off shakes me out of Sabre's grasp. I list severely to the side, balanced on the terrifying precipice, watching horror fill Sabre's eyes as I topple off.

For several seconds, I'm in freefall, the coats that Hattie gave me fluttering around my ears like a leaf caught in a gale. For a moment or two, it's difficult to tell I'm falling. The updraft battles with the downstroke from one of Herrick's wings and I tumble sideways and down. Then gravity finally catches hold of me in its iron fist and drags me abruptly downward. I think I shriek, but even the sound is whipped away too quickly to be heard. The wind seems to reach icy fingers down my throat and freeze my lungs solid, so I can't even draw in breath enough for the next scream.

Distantly, I can hear others yelling. Draven's voice, higher than normal, Sabre's cutting across him in a rebuke I can't hear and then…

A dark shape hurtles into me from the side, enormous scaly talons closing around my waist.

There's a moment where I'm afraid the keen, pointed edges will cut me to ribbons and send the slurry to slap the earth. It doesn't happen. Instead, the talons flex around me, holding me longways so the wind whips my face, but is unable to pluck the rest of me from the air.

I crane my neck to get a look at my rescuer. It's one of the huntsmen, that's for certain. The profile is avian and unfamiliar. Not Sabre's beautifully patterned jay's head. Nor is it a raven's stately profile, so this can't be Draven's beast form either. The feathers are a beautiful tawny, underlain with black. He looks like a stunning mix between a red-tailed hawk and a raven, except for the head and neck. There's a tufted pile of down around his neck, like he's donned a fur coat, and his neck is a slender, gray column. The beak is cruelly tapered, the eyes set above it a vivid, terrifying red. The eyes of a vulture. Gryphus.

Titus, or Gatz? Which has a hold of me now?

Either way, we're hurtling toward the ground in a controlled dive, rather than plummeting straight down as I had been before. Herrick hadn't gotten us far enough off the ground for the save and ascension to be easy. The best my rescuer can manage is to keep my fall from being fatal. Further evidence this is Titus, not Gatz, but I still can't ease the knot of terror in my gut just yet. Not until I see his face, feel his body around mine.

We hit the tops of a colorful wonderland wood a moment later, thankfully near a clearing, so my general person is only mildly thrashed instead of bludgeoned by a sea of branches. The break in the trees barely accommodates the shifter's massive wingspan, and he lets out a sound of pain as his wingtips are ripped at by the branches of the trees as we land.

He releases me when we're a foot off the ground, so he won't crush me beneath his bulk. I land on my back, still far enough from the ground that the impact knocks the breath out of me. I'm only able to manage an uncoordinated roll to get clear of his path before I have to still my aching body. Talons pierce the ground near my head, steadying the enormous bird, and a heavy wing drapes over my body, either shielding me in order to hide me, or else to keep me safe from attackers.

It leaves me spinning in the relative dark, feeling as though I'm about to be sucked down an enormous drain and into the void beyond. There isn't a part of me that doesn't hurt. Ringing begins in my ears, and my eyes slide shut.

I feel so suddenly tired. But, I know I can't fall asleep.

Don't fall asleep…

But the darkness seizes me anyway, and I lose precious seconds, possible minutes before I come back to myself again. I'm once more cradled in a man's arms and we're running. Or rather... we're trying to run. His gait is sloppy, lurching like some sort of cursed revenant in the pursuit of flesh. The barrel chest I'm clutched against heaves with effort and if I strain my ears, I can hear the strangest noise. It's like... enormous giant's feet crashing through the trees. But that can't be right, can it? The giants have been extinct for many years, with the exception of Morningstar and his ilk, right?

Light slants through the trees at odd intervals and I peer with difficulty through my lashes. The man holding me is completely naked, sweat gleaming off every available inch of skin. My breath comes easier when I see the strong, familiar profile, the dark hair, and the streak of off-center red.

"Titus," I breathe. "Where are we? What's that noise?"

"It's the church," he huffs. "The fucking bastards spelled it to *walk*."

EIGHTEEN
TITUS

We're so damn close to the border.

And I still don't think we're going to make it.

Some of the Wonderland vegetation can simply uproot itself and flee as the church approaches. It makes my task damn near impossible. The stretch of land we're in doesn't have so much as a footpath cut into the ground, and the fleeing flora and fauna only muddy the issue. A shape that looks like a multi-hued fox gets its tail wedged beneath my boot as we both flee from the oncoming building.

"Sorry, little fox!" I yell, but it's too late. It's already gone.

When I return my eyes in the direction I've been running, it's almost too late to stop myself from bowling over the stem of a giant, overturned Morel plant. Fortunately, the stem is spongy and I ricochet off, with only my pride stinging this time.

The rest of me stings a whole hell of a lot. Every spare nettle, thistle, and briar has found my skin in the minutes I've jogged with Carmine in my arms. I'm bleeding from about three dozen or so cuts and my feet will be only so much meat by the time I reach the border of the Anoka Desert.

If I reach the border.

Carmine gasps, craning her neck to peer over my shoulder. I can't tell, but I'm just willing to bet those big quicksilver eyes have gone wide. Maybe her mouth is hanging open too. Mine sure as fuck was when the cellar-level of the church merely shrugged off the layer of dirt that held the foundations in place and reached eight spider-like legs from the hole and stood up. That first step it took nearly pulverized me.

My right arm is screaming from the effort of trying to support her weight. On a good day, the one-hundred-twenty pound girl wouldn't trouble me, but with all the fingers of my hand and most the ones in my wrist snapped like twigs, grinding together as I move, it's all I can do not to throw up. I keep moving out of sheer recalcitrance, as Sabre would say. I won't let myself be done in by a fucking *house,* mechanical legs on it be damned. I won't be like the tale from a far-off land where a witch was crushed by a farmhouse.

One of the church's clawed feet impacts the ground only a half-mile behind us. Its stride is incredibly long. In no time at all, it will close the distance and then we're fucked. Where have my brothers and those damn dragons disappeared to? Taking Neva away, writing Carmine and I as lost causes?

No, I can't believe that. Draven, at the very least, would cut off his own balls before he'd let any harm come to her. There has to be another battle going on elsewhere. Perhaps those damn maenads are still attacking Herrick. Yes, that has to be it.

"Titus, put me down," Carmine says quietly.

I almost don't catch her voice over the whipping of the wind in my ears and the excited clicking sounds issuing not far behind us. I know it's the spider-legged dark fae that stood on the dais. If I'd been in bird form, I'd have been able to snap it up in my beak, scissoring it in two. If it had been an oversized spider, I'd have swallowed it in all likelihood. But knowing it's dark fae, I'd have to spit it out. Dead fae are unpredictable creatures, Seelie or Unseelie. The magic still imbues the flesh, dead or alive... shit could get strange fast. I hear they cut the pixie dust from the corpse of the Blue Faerie into drugs these days.

"No," I grind out. It's a real effort not to scream.

"Titus, please. It's going to keep following us and then Bacchus' revelry will know we're coming."

"Doesn't matter!"

"I think I can stop it, Titus. Give me a chance."

I should just keep going, but there's something about her wheedling tone... I can't deny her.

I pause, cursing every second we're stationary and set her gingerly on her feet. She sways, still a little shaky after the rough landing we took. She plants her feet a little apart, steels herself, and sets her jaw in determination. She's ruffled, her clothing ripped in places, and she's bleeding. My libido doesn't care. For the second time since she joined us, I see the hints of a warrior queen peeking out from beneath the soft veneer of a demure princess.

If only we could find a way to strip away all the propriety and leave the core of steel beneath. She has it in her. She knows what she wants, at least in bed. She is sure and confident. I could make her a warrior, given time. She could at least be as tough as Kassidy. But we have to live through this to get there. I pray to the Gods she knows what she's doing.

Carmine kneels, placing a palm flat on the ground. Her eyes flutter closed and a strange calm seems to come over her. Words, in a language I've never heard, flow from her mouth, tumbling over each other like the sound of running water. It's mesmerizing and I stand, trance-like, watching the little witchling, our little Chosen One for a second longer than I should.

Then the twitching shape of the spider-like dark fae bursts onto the footpath, leaping down from the mushroom head nearest us.

It isn't alone. Gatz is riding on its back, arms locked around its torso. He looks faintly nauseous and clambers off as fast as he can. The thing's skin must feel as revolting as it appears. His avian form is as useless as mine in these close quarters.

There's a blade in my hand before I even consciously think of it. I'm not as good with my left, never learning the skill equally with both hands, the way Draven and Sabre did. The shortsword is my least favorite weapon. Give me a shuriken, a chakkar, a scythe on a chain. Anything, but this fucking thing. Of course, I am left to do melee with Gatz, who's possibly one of the best swordsmen the Order of Aves has ever seen. That's not even counting the threat of the spider-fae.

Fate loves to stick it up my ass... dry.

I hope Carmine knows what the fuck she's doing, because I'm not sure how long I'll be able to defend her against both. She's still murmuring and, like before, things begin to sprout from the ground. Drecaine vines slither over the barely worn path like verdant snakes, choking out the ferns and thistles that litter the ground here. Gatz and the spider edge away from them with sharp sounds of panic. Carmine isn't paying them any mind. Her eyes snap open, and the silver sheens her sclera now, giving her the look of a proper night hag.

A prickle of fear eases up my spine, adding to the already potent unease I'm feeling. A byproduct of her magic. There's more night hag in her than I dreamed. God help me if she goes full night hag in this clearing. She could turn on me as easily as Gatz or the dark fae.

For now, her focus is on the approaching church and the couple of fae that ride atop the roof. It's so near now, I can see the pair of conjoined fae swinging from a busted out window. They're dangling the priest out the window, their joined tail forming a sort of noose. He must have pissed them off in some way.

The snaking vines reach the foot of the nearest leg and wind around the claw-like foot. It reaches another leg a few moments later and I finally cotton on to her plan. Clever, clever girl.

We don't need to destroy the church, just slow it down or take it out of commission. Tipping it will do nicely. Unfortunately, I'm not the only one who's had the revelation. Gatz's eyes burn with hate and fix on Carmine. His blade is out as well, flashing what light is to be had into my eyes in a calculated move to blind me.

"You get the girl," he hisses at the dark fae. "I'll deal with my dear cousin."

My stomach lurches violently, and I teeter on the verge of throwing up again. This is exactly the scenario I've been attempting to avoid. Gatz is a deluded, short-sighted bastard, but he wasn't always a villainous asshole. I don't want to kill him. I also don't see other options.

The spider is moving, faster than a crossbow bolt, the disquieting clicking echoing along the narrow footpath. I don't have long to consider. It's a trap and I damn well know it. If I go for the spider, I open flank to Gatz, who will gut me. If I don't, Carmine will be dead in a matter of seconds. This type of dark fae likes to rip heads off and drink from the stump of the neck.

There's no choice at all, really.

I pivot, placing my body between Carmine and the charging dark fae, thrusting the blade at the point where a heart should logically be on a human torso. Who the fuck knows if it will have any effect on the dark fae. They could keep their hearts in their assholes, for all I know.

It backpedals a step, and the thrust misses. The mouthless face slits open with a wet slurp of sound to reveal a set of large mandibles. They snap shut on my blade, almost wrenching the whole thing from my grasp. Fuck.

With a grunt, I'm able to free it, slashing a bloody streak across one side of its face, but the tip breaks off, leaving it useless for thrusting cleanly. This blade isn't good for slashing, but I'll just have to try. With a vicious curse, I take a page from Carmine's book and bring the blade down on one of the spider's legs. It doesn't take the thing off completely, but it hangs as limp and useless as my broken hand.

It's enough to slow the thing down, make it cringe away in pain. I don't have time to deliver the killing blow, however.

If Gatz hadn't had the fatal flaw of announcing his attacks with a grunt, I'd have been a dead man. As it is, I'm only able to keep the blade from parting my head from my shoulders. The blade cuts neatly through the tail at the base of my neck at an angle and my head feels a little lighter as the hair tumbles to the ground. A brief flicker of irritation consumes me. Petty and vain, yes, but I liked my hair, damn it. So did women.

No choice. No fucking choice.

It's him or me, him or Carmine. But it fucking hurts. Why does it hurt so fucking badly? I *knew* this could happen. I just didn't know it would be *me* delivering the death blow.

The punch I deliver to his diaphragm is a favorite move of Sabre's. One good punch and you could freeze the muscles there for just a second or two. More than enough time to slide a knife into the heart. Real fear bleeds into Gatz's eyes when he realizes what I've done, realizes the shortsword, even a broken one, is enough to end him for good.

But... I can't.

I can't fucking kill him. Even to save me. Even to save her. I can't slide a blade into his heart and watch the light leave his eyes.

I thrust it into his thigh instead, pinning him to the ground. The blow takes him down to one knee and he lets out a porcine shriek of pain as I drive the metal to the hilt. There are large arteries in the leg. Maybe I've killed him. Maybe I haven't. But it's a damn sight better than ending him like a felled buck. There's still a chance for him.

I seize Gatz's shoulders, whipping his coat off as best as I can. It's heavy, loaded up with weaponry, precisely what I was hoping for. Mine was lost the moment I had to shift. The fabric tears in places, but doesn't slide off my shoulders when I shrug it on. There. Protection from the elements and weaponry.

The spider is hissing mad, spitting some sort of acid onto the ground. It sizzles through some of the drecaine vines that have pulled taut. A few of them snap, but not enough to halt the inevitable result.

Three of the church's mechanical legs go out from under it. It tips slowly backward, with a groan of protest, launching the remaining dark fae off the roof. I can't tell if the building crushes them as it topples. The impact shakes the ground, every tree and mushroom in the area shaking.

I can barely focus on it, even the flame of pride I feel doused by horror as what I've done catches up to me.

Gatz is still wailing.

His blood has splashed onto my bare skin. Oh Gods, what have I done?

I punch him hard enough at just the right point to knock him unconscious. Better for him that way.

Distantly, I see Carmine stand at last, turning her attention to the dark fae. The silver is spreading out from her eyes, black tears slipping down her cheeks. The darkness pools on her skin, spreads. Her lips are turning violet.

Fuck, she's going full night hag. Even the spider knows better than to face down a Chosen One who's losing control. It scuttles away as fast as its good legs will allow. Carmine's dispassionate eyes track it with the speculative hunger of a lion on the hunt. Her tongue flicks out to trace one violet lip, tasting the fear on the air, savoring it.

"Carmine," I croak. "Carmine, we need to go."

Her head swivels to face me in an almost serpentine motion. It's damn eerie, and I shrink back a step. With the silver gaze turned on me, I feel the hot sluice of blood all the more acutely. Every wretched emotion rises to choke the breath from me.

There's something horribly compelling about her still.

Dark beauty, but beauty nonetheless. I never understood why Leon married the plain Salome, with her wicked other half. Now I understand a little better. This is the magic of the night hag, the feared *mora,* the nightmare made flesh. This power would compel a man to let the crazy bitches to crouch over his chest and steal the sanity from him.

"Titus," she murmurs. There's a new resonance to her voice. Deeper and echoing, like it's coming from the bottom of a well. "Titus I feel... strange."

"You need to feed," I say, barely able to keep the tremor from my voice. "You've used your powers too much in a short stretch. No training and... God, have you fed it at all, your whole life?"

"Fed what?" She sounds genuinely bemused. That would be a 'no' then.

I can't fucking do this. I won't let her dredge up my worst memories and drink them down like so much Sweetland port. It'd be fucking terrifying for me and the Princess will hate herself when she wakes from this insanity. But what else is there to do? Night hags are only consumed with two things. Fear and violence. I can't very well attack her or allow her to attack me.

"You look so... good," she murmurs, licking her violet lips again. "Smell so good. I want to taste you. Feel you in my mouth."

"So most women say," I respond, unable to help the quip even as she glides closer, the aura of malevolence growing every passing second.

Then the thought really penetrates. I'm not sure I want that violet mouth on my cock (at this juncture, at any rate) but if I could subdue her harshly enough, fuck her roughly enough... would it be enough to satisfy the hunger for fear and blood?

I shrug off the coat after a moment of consideration and draw myself up to my full height. I'm bloodied, one hand broken, my hair is probably lopsided from Gatz's unintentional role as barber. Still, she ca"t seem to take her eyes off my chest. If I hadn't known better, I might have thought her one of the blood drinkers.

"Want this?" I say, pointing at my cock and stuffing as much bravado as I can into the taunt. "You think you can take me, Princess?"

"I want you," she repeats, tracking the line of blood from one pectoral down to my navel. She looks at it the way I've had women study my cock. Like she wants to swallow me whole.

"Do you want to fuck me? Bloody me?"

A moan catches in her throat and I can see her nipples tauten even beneath the coat she wears. Despite myself, I want a taste. I've been fucking curious since the night she touched herself for me.

Breasts are my gift. I wonder if I can make her climax touching them alone?

"Gods, yes."

I'm not sure who moves first, but within three steps we meet in a tangle of thrashing limbs. She has small claws that I've never seen on her before, still more of her night hag biology peeking out. They score marks on my abdomen. Her mouth latches onto my neck the instant she's in range and she rubs her body catlike against mine. Fear and anticipation do battle in my head. I don't think I've had a more confusing hard-on in my life.

My hands move, almost on instinct, as though I've been waiting to do this since the moment we met. Around her waist, digging my fingers in hard. I can't let the fear show, can't show weakness in front of her. Weakness makes me prey, and prey gets eaten. She'll gobble up my sanity and possibly end my life right along with it. So I dig my nails in until they've carved bloody crescents into her skin, holding her as tightly as I can, exerting all my beast's strength. She'll have bad bruises by tomorrow morning, but she doesn't seem to care. The force draws a protracted moan from her throat. My cock strains toward her, unperturbed by the chill of coming dusk. I grind it into her front.

She struggles with her clothing and with a bestial snarl, I tear her top from hemline to bodice. It draws a startled gasp from her. I shove it and the coat off her as quickly as I can. Her arousal is drowning the acrid scent of my fear. If I slide my fingers between her legs, they'll come away wet. Soaking. That's gratifying. And wrong. Draven will kill me for fucking his woman. On the other hand, I don't think he'll be too pleased with her if she murders me in an out-of-control feeding either.

When her eyes meet mine, the silver is so goddamn mesmerizing, it takes my breath away. She looks like some sort of goddess, with those swirling quicksilver eyes, those scarlet curls standing around her head like a bloody halo around her breathtaking face. She looks carved out of ivory.

"Titus, please."

"Please what?"

"I want pain. Fear. Blood."

I slide my hands up her back, shove one into her hair like I did that evening in the clearing and bring my lips down on hers in a crushing kiss. I drag her lower lip between my teeth, worrying it until the tang of blood fills my mouth. I'm afraid I've done too much, but she moans, winds herself around me. I edge her backward, forcing her into a rhythm like we're in a savage sort of dance. I don't stop until her back hits the hard trunk of a tufted yellow and blue barked tree. She impacts so hard, the violet leaves above us shudder.

I undress her quickly, easily.

"Titus," she gasps.

I stroke my fingers along the underside of her breasts. Small and pert. Her nipples are rosy, peaked, and dying for my attention. I stroke one lovingly and trail kisses across her jaw, down her neck, and across her collarbone until I find the swell of it. I nip her skin, drawing another gasp from her, then press my teeth in harder, until I leave the imprint on her skin. She's flushed now, panting for air.

I lick along the swell of her breasts, down, until I reach a puckered nipple. She lets out a sharp cry, arching her back hard when I latch on, giving her just an edge of teeth as I lavish attention on it. Part of me wishes she had a piercing or two here, the way some of the strumpets in Grimm do. The texture is something else, and I could add a layer of pleasure by tugging them, giving her some more of the pain she so clearly craves.

"Harder," she pleads. I hesitate. "Please, Titus."

I tighten my grip. Her pale skin will be littered with bruises by this point. I don't think either of us care. She's mewling, almost crying with pleasure as I lavish attention on first one breast and then the other. Her hips roll, brushing my cock on every revolution until I'm teetering on that edge as well.

"No," I grind out. I am not orgasming on her thigh like some hormonal teen with his first lover. I want to be seated between her thighs, fucking her until her legs give out.

"Please," she whines. "I need you… inside me, Titus."

I release her breast after a few more seconds of teasing, trailing my fingers down her body, sliding just the tip of my finger between her folds. Her bud is swollen, ready with need and she lets out a half-sob when I feather easy strokes over it. I keep at it until tears actually stream down her face. Clear, human tears, instead of the black of her night hag form. It's working. She's becoming more herself. A less selfish man would bring her to orgasm with his fingers and let it be done.

I've never claimed to be unselfish.

I sling first one leg and then the other around my waist. She clings on, urging me forward with little nudges at the small of my back. The tip of my cock slides through her slick folds and I sink, inch by inch, into the warmth of her pussy. It's my turn to bite back a moan. She clamps down on my cock hard, almost as if she's unwilling to let go. Her hips buck into mine and again, it's all I can do not to spill inside her.

Bracing my hand near the side of her face, I rock my hips into hers, thrusting experimentally.

"Harder," she pants.

I draw back and thrust in as hard as I can and she screams. She screams so loud and long, I'm almost sure any survivors from the church will find us and end us. Nothing comes bursting from the underbrush to attack us, but even so, I claim her mouth in an almost bruising kiss to muffle the sound. Her moans trickle into my mouth instead, and it's so fucking hot, I can't fucking think straight.

I pump into her, over and over again, rutting her like an animal. Bestial grunts escape me, screams escape her, muffled by my mouth. She only clutches me tighter, pulls me in closer, scoring my back with those wicked nails. No longer claws, thank the Gods. But still, the sensation is incredible.

Her back bows into a perfect arch and her walls flutter around me in a tell-tale sign before she comes, clenching down hard. My own release comes a few seconds later. We stay like that for a second, maybe two, staring at each other. Unspoken truth crackles between us.

We shouldn't have done it, no matter how badly we wanted to. Draven will be fucking livid. What's more, I spilled inside her. What the fuck will we do if she gets pregnant?

I slide out of her and she winces, finally coming back to herself. She's fully human now. Good. Crisis averted.

"Titus..." she begins, then falls silent. She doesn't know what to say. Frankly, I don't either.

"Let's get going," I pant, picking up what remains of her clothing.

She nods.

NINETEEN
CARMINE

It takes us ten minutes to find the others.

Ten minutes in which I have to ponder my rash decision.

I can barely recall anything but desire. Desire for blood, desire for *him*. I feel wretched, even as a pleasant ache radiates between my thighs. It's almost as if I can still feel Titus between my legs. He'd been more beast than man as he fucked me against the tree.

And I'd loved it. Even thinking about it now makes desire coil tight in my belly. I hope Titus doesn't smell it. Perhaps it's masked by the scent of the sex we've just had.

But there was more—I felt something dark taking over me, something roaring through my body that scared me. And Titus... he was able to stop it. He was able to help me control myself by giving me his body. I still don't fully understand how or why, but the fact remains.

I can't stop thinking of him. Can't stop imagining what it might be like to be taken by him again, from behind this time, with him tugging my hair.

Stop it, I snap at myself. *What is wrong with you, Carmine? What will Draven say?*

Thoughts of Draven instantly douse whatever lust I'm feeling for Titus. Oh Gods above, he's never going to forgive me for this, is he? Not so long ago I was pining for him, *only* for him. And now that I've been his, I'm leaping into the arms of his brothers. And regardless of whether or not they are truly related, they are brothers, all the same.

I'm almost afraid to step out to meet the others. Their voices filter to us through the mushroom forest. Low, anxious. Neva's is almost strident, balancing between a shriek and a sob. She's begging someone to take her back. Where to? I'm not sure. Up ahead, I can see a slice of brilliant whiteness cutting through the gloom. It takes me a few seconds to realize it's the moon reflecting off pristine white dunes. Shadows puddle between them, violet against the pale expanse. It's strikingly beautiful. Almost stark when contrasted with the riot of colors that is the Wonderland landscape. I'm grateful for it. I'm sick of all the chaos.

I frown. Now that isn't really true is it? If I want less chaos, I shouldn't add men into my bed and on a whim.

Titus emerges from the forest first and I follow close behind, almost hiding in his shadow. Cowardly, cowardly Carmine. There is no way in Avernus I can be Chosen. I can barely scrounge up the courage to look the man I love in the eyes and admit what I've done. With his brother.

Every eye swivels our direction, relief sponging the mixed panic and anger from the faces of all assembled. Neva lurches from Reve's arms and launches herself at me, arms flung wide. She almost sends us both to the ground with the force of her embrace. I can't bring myself to pull away from her when she wraps me in an enormous hug and squeezes me for all she's worth.

"Gods, I thought I'd lost you!" she sobs, almost hiccupping the words. They're coming through tears now. "Don't ever scare me like that again!"

"I won't," I mumble. "And I'm sorry."

To my surprise, Sabre drags me in for an embrace the second Neva releases me. His arms are stronger, holding me more securely to his chest. There's a tremor running through his body.

"Forgive me, Carmine," he whispers. "I didn't mean to..."

"Don't worry, Sabre. Titus caught me."

Only then does Sabre draw in breath and when he does, he stiffens. I cringe inwardly. Titus' scent must be thick on my skin. If Sabre can smell it, Draven most certainly can. Sabre draws away slowly, a pensive look on his face. My heart sinks a little further.

Gods, what have I done?

"We heard a crash," Herrick says, craning his neck back toward the Wonderland forest. "What happened?"

"Carmine tangled with the legs of the church. It's down for good and most of the fae were killed or fled," Titus explains. Then he turns to look at me. "She was amazing."

Maybe I'm imagining it, but I think I hear a double entendre in that statement. My cheeks flame, in any case. I stare at the sand at my feet, unable to take the praise, knowing what I did immediately after. What we did. I can feel eyes on me, one set in particular heavier than the others combined. I don't want to look. I think I'd rather stare at the sand the whole way to the Anoka mountains than see the look of anger or worse, profound disappointment on Draven's face.

"Carmine."

One word.

His voice is soft.

His boots enter my field of vision and his gentle fingers tug my chin up. My vision hazes. When had I started crying? I struggle to swallow around the lump in my throat.

His face is sweet, some unknown emotion in his eyes, but I don't see condemnation.

"I'm sorry," I mumble. "I'm sorry. I just... the other half of me emerged. The night hag and..."

Draven's mouth covers mine in a tender kiss, cutting off my babbled explanation. He coaxes my lips open and takes me, tastes me until I'm breathless and the tears have stopped. He strokes the side of my face with his thumb.

"Don't," he murmurs. "Don't cry, Carmine. I told you. If you want him, you can have him."

"It's not fair to any of you," I mutter.

"Any or all of us are lucky to have you. Stop castigating yourself. We can't have you mired in guilt when the time comes to fight."

"But…"

"I love you, Carmine. I always will. But that doesn't mean others can't love you too."

I stare up into his face, stunned by the naked and unwavering devotion he's showing me. Gods, how did I ever get him? I don't deserve him.

"We don't have time for this,' Malvolo snaps impatiently.

His dark eyes are fixed on a faraway point. I follow it, not catching sight of his target for almost a minute. All I can see are the dunes, a pattern of waving white sand and dark shadows. The mountains loom in the distant, a byzantine purple almost blending with the dark, spangled banner of the sky.

Then I spot it. A small pinprick of orange light at the base of the tallest peak. It flickers, and I see a host of black shapes flitting around it, like moths drawn to a flame.

"What is it?" I ask.

"Bacchus' revelry," Sabre says, and for the first time, I hear a hint of his beast in his voice. There's a note of gravelly bass undercutting his words.

My pulse speeds, and I can practically taste my anxiety in my throat. All the illicit pleasure from the clearing is gone, the guilt a pale echo of itself. This is what we've been searching for. Our goal is perhaps only a few days' walk away. A shorter trip still if we fly. The answers to saving our people could be within our grasp very soon, indeed.

So why do I want to flee back into the damn forest?

"What's our plan?" I ask, daring a glance toward the rest of our band.

Neva's men huddle around her, each with a hand on her somewhere. Herrick braces her shoulders. Malvolo has a hand on her ass. Reve's hand rests just above on the small of her back. Hattie and Ia stand a little way off, stark contrasts to each other. Hattie is a patchwork of color. A red velvet top hat, a green overcoat, yellow shirt, brown breeches, and striped stockings stuffed into penny loafers.

Ia is an amalgam of greys. Slate hair, ashy pale skin, a tunic the color of pewter, similar breeches and calf-high boots. She looks like a literal shadow standing next to Hattie.

"We fly," Ia says simply. "A little camouflage will be necessary. I assume you can oblige, Ms. Trilby?"

Hattie smiles for the first time since leaving her home, the lopsided grin gleeful and utterly, utterly mad. "Of course," she purrs. "I live to play dress up. Could our dear little birdies shift for me please?"

The huntsmen exchange uneasy glances.

"Why do I have a bad feeling about this?" Draven grumbles, reaching for the hem of his shirt.

"Because she's fucking batty," Titus answers. He has an easier time of it, simply shrugging off the coat, letting it pool on the ground like a scarlet bloodstain.

But I find my attention fixed on Sabre, insatiable curiosity making me peer more closely. He's the only one I haven't seen nude. A glance at him when he divests himself of his trousers makes my throat go dry. Good Gods.

Sabre cuts a glare to Hattie that would cause me to shrink away from him. Her enthusiasm doesn't dim.

"You better not turn us into toads or something," he warns.

"Not toads," she assures him with a manic grin. "Rocs."

TWENTY
SABRE

Hattie's glamour makes my skin itch.

I dislike the tan and beige appearance of my wings. I miss the vibrant blue and black pattern. I don't know how Titus fucking stands the bland colors.

Hattie digs her heels more firmly into my sides, even as we glide above the sands. The sand is cooling rapidly as the night progresses. During the day, the thermals resulting from the desert heat would be phenomenal. As it is, I'm having to work hard to keep myself and my passengers aloft.

I drew the short end of the stick and am carrying the two mad witches on my back.

"Stop complaining, jay," Hattie clucks. "This is working, is it not?"

I grimace inwardly. The second component of the fucking spell was necessary, but irritating. Loud thoughts or thoughts directed at an individual allowed my brothers and I to coordinate. It also made it easy for the mad bitch to eavesdrop, especially when making contact with my bare back.

Still, I can't deny the effectiveness of the spell. Not a single one of the archers we've passed are trying to fell us with arrows. They know better. The Rocs are a feared bird from a kingdom across the Anoka desert. Even Bacchus won't risk attacking the Rocs, won't risk their retribution. Not when his infiltration is already going so well.

The Church of the Seven Joys had been cropping up like weeds in every kingdom in Fantasia, excluding the cordoned off portion guarded by Maura LeChance. They've been here for a few years, slowly amassing power and we'd never suspected.

Were we blind or were they simply that good? Neither bodes well for our fate in the coming war.

The camp is nearer now, and what had once looked like a pinprick of light on the horizon has resolved itself into a massive bonfire. The scent of spirits rides the wind, so strong it makes my eyes cross. The wine at Bacchus' revelries never stops flowing. Chalices brim with it, spilling to the ground during spirited jigs or when one of the maenads is taken to the ground to be rutted by a libidinous satyr or centaur. Fucking and fighting and sheer, uncontrolled chaos reigns wherever Bacchus goes. The magic is so potent, it often lures humans, who are either crushed or fucked to death during the unending merriment.

I squeeze my eyes shut for a half second as I try to keep the pictures from flitting to the forefront of my mind. I don't want to relive them, and I don't want to broadcast them to Neva, Carmine, or the dragon generals. But they come anyway.

"Gods," Carmine breathes as she faces me. "Gods, Sabre, I'm so sorry."

Shit. I haven't kept the memories to myself. I've broadcasted them for all to see—the death of my mother.

"We're nearly there," Draven says in a tone that's meant to be cavalier. Linked as we are, I know it's a lie. His stomach is roiling, faint nausea tinging his thoughts. *"This can end tonight. We'll land, dance our way through, and we'll get the stones. Bacchus' people will never know what happened. At least, not until the revelry ends."*

"That could be hours or days away," I think in response.

He nods. *"Enough time to get the fuck out of here."*

It sounds simple, though we know it will be anything but. Even if we make it to Bacchus' camp undetected, we still have to blend with the crowd. Difficult, when Hattie and Ia are so instantly recognizable. Draven, Titus, and I can mask our scent with the mud or blood that's sure to be thick on the ground. But Carmine? Even with a glamour, she's damn distinctive. The recent emergence of her night hag self makes her reek of blood, death, and fear. I miss her floral scent. It'll come back in a few days, I believe, but until then? It's not going to go unnoticed.

Bacchus' revelries only result in the fear of the victims and so far as we can tell from this distance, there don't appear to be any around Mount Vallis. The desert people are nomadic and had there been any, I think they'd have had the good sense to get the fuck out when Bacchus' revelry approached them.

"Ia, Hattie, and Carmine will stay on the periphery while the rest of us proceed into the camp," Draven continues.

There's a wave of mutinous denial from Carmine.

"I'm going."

Her voice sounds distant and tiny through the roar of the wind, but I still hear it.

"No the fuck you are not," Titus growls. *"You'll only get yourself killed."*

"I'm a Chosen One. If I'm not built to do this, what good am I?"

"You're good, Carmine, but not this *good. You need training. We can't have you getting killed,"* Draven says, trying to smooth her ruffled feathers. *"A dead Chosen One is no good to anyone."*

It doesn't work. Out of the corner of one eye, I see her fold her arms beneath her breasts, glaring down at Draven's sleek, dark head. Somehow the muted colors suit him more.

"Neva is going."

"Neva has had training and can shift into whatever she damn well pleases. She can even mask her own scent. You can't. Stay with Hattie and Ia."

"That is such tripe," she snaps. "I can go. Just let me…"

"No." All three of us say in chorus.

Carmine's lip juts in a petulant pout, and even though my focus should be on the upcoming mission, I can't help but think what it might be like to tug that lip between my teeth.

A flash of hot desire sears across my awareness and I have a brief glimpse of a reciprocal vision. Carmine laid out beneath all of us, taking a fair amount of pain with her pleasure, drinking in the illicit thrill of it. The thought of being filled so fully has her painfully aroused. She shifts on Draven's back uncomfortably. I'm more than a little pleased to know I'm in her fantasies.

Neva is just behind her sister, and I catch the scrunch of her pert little nose.

"Thanks, sis. Really needed the visual."

It's hard to tell in the midnight dark, but I think a light dusting of pink coats Carmine's cheeks.

"Sorry."

"Hush, all of you," Ia snaps. "We're nearly there. Let's not alert them."

Chastised, we all fall silent. The wind whistles beneath my feathers, cool and stinking of spirits. We're nearly on them now. We circle slowly, keeping out of the glow of the bonfire as best we can. The flames dance almost twelve feet tall, and scattered before it is a revelry. A small one, compared to the one that sacked our hometown. Are we fortunate or about to be made fools? I can't help but feel this has to be a trap. Morningstar wouldn't leave the cache so lightly guarded. Even with an ego to match his giant's size, I don't think he could be that stupid.

A particularly high dune provides us with enough cover to shift back to our human forms. As soon as our passengers land safely on the sand, I'm shrinking down, eagerly retaking the bipedal form. Anything to get that itchy glamour off my skin. The mental connection will remain, though less potent now that we have tongues to speak with.

Another wave of arousal hits me like a fist to the chest, knocking the wind out of me. A glance at Carmine shows me her attention isn't on my face. She's studying my cock with fascination. If I press, I can feel the momentary thought of having it inside of her.

"Later," I murmur. "For now, there's work to be done."

"Right," she says, cheeks very pink now. It will never cease being cute, no matter how dire the situation.

She offers me a bundle of clothes, which I accept gratefully. The desert is growing more icy by the minute. Perhaps that's the reason for the unreasonably large bonfire. To stop the maenads and the rest from freezing their tits or balls off. The sand that shifts beneath my toes is lukewarm at best, the air sweeping off Mount Vallis is colder. It cuts through the layers of clothing like blades. I grit my teeth against the cold. It'll be a lot warmer where we're going. I can take an hour of this before we infiltrate. A little observation will save our lives. It's worth losing a testicle to save all of Fantasia from Morningstar's machinations.

When we're all dressed, we creep closer, cresting the dune with difficulty until we can peer over. The vantage point gives us a good overview of the camp. The bonfire is the central point, and figures range out from it. The maenads are nearest to the center, twisting in an utterly indecent dance before a pair of shapes.

I don't think the man is Bacchus. Not fat enough, for one. The brief glimpses of him I'd gotten during the last war showed him to be a gourmand, twice as wide as he was tall, with hair that hung in greasy strings down his back and shoulders. Beady little eyes, a nose like a squashed tomato.

But still, these gods or goddesses aren't to be trifled with, if Morningstar's generals have left them in charge.

Ia pops her head up beside mine and examines the inner circle as well.

"Deianira and one of her lovers," she says, almost seeming to echo my thoughts. "Bacchus' daughter. Very powerful."

"Any way to stop her?"

"Do you happen to have a bull's horn handy?"

"No."

"I could be one," Neva says, cropping up on my other side.

"Won't work," Ia answers. "Has to be the genuine article, dear, not the rearranged molecules of a Chosen One."

"Well, fuck."

"Deianira can be injured any number of ways, but not killed without it."

"As much as I hate to say it, we don't need them dead," Titus says, settling his weight on the top of the ridge, peering down with contempt at the revelers. "We just need the stones. It's safer if we don't charge in with the intent to slaughter."

It goes against every promise we've ever made ourselves. The fuckers are laid out before us, helpfully illuminated by a massive fire. All it would take is a supply of arrows and a good crossbow to end the whole sorry lot of them. They're like fish in a barrel. It wouldn't even be sporting.

Titus is right.

And if the most impulsive member of our band can swallow the desire to slaughter them, I'll do my best to swallow my pride and go along with the plan.

Or at least, that's what I tell myself as I scan the rest of their number. The second ring of revelers is made up of a thin band of dark fae, the third composed of satyrs and the high priests and priestesses of the cult. The fourth is made up of rutting centaurs, fucking what look to be a few captured women repeatedly. One in particular stands out. A beefy fellow, with a chestnut cast to his skin, the pelt of a red roan, and a swishing tail the same black as the stuff on his head. His raucous laughter reaches my ears, even a half-mile away.

It's the same laugh I heard all those years ago, when the revelry was in full sway, trampling everyone and everything in its path.

And that's when the white hiss of sound fills my ears, my mind going blank with only one single thought scrolling across my mind.

Kill. Kill. Kill.

Because I've been searching for him for years, this creature. It's been my life's ambition to end him, and I'm not about to let him go. Not now. Not that he's finally within my sight.

I launch myself over the dune, sliding down into the shadowy valley between, that same thought beating a tattoo against my skull.

I'm going to kill Arcadius.

Our original plan be damned.

TWENTY-ONE
CARMINE

"Oh, fuck," Titus says, words low but fervent. "That fucking moron."

I, for one, can't stop staring at Sabre's retreating back. What in the name of Avernus has possessed him to run into the revelry?

"We have to stop him!" I hiss.

"He'll ruin everything!" Draven says.

"What's gotten into the crazy bastard?" Malvolo mutters. "Wasn't he the one advocating for taking it slow not so long ago?"

"Fuck," Draven says. "It's Arcadius. He's here."

That name dredges up a faint recollection. Me, sitting on Sabre's lap not long after making love to Draven. Sabre telling me about his mother's assault, the origin behind the feather he keeps in his braid. It's coated in deadly poison, on the off chance that he ever runs across his mother's murderer. And now Sabre's found him. No wonder he's gone off script.

"What do we do?" I ask, not sure if I'm seeking an answer from the others, or simply trying to puzzle it all out for myself.

"Nothing for it," Draven mutters. "We have to go in after him. Neva, shift to blend. Hattie, go with the generals and whip up another glamour spell. Just a thin veneer will work. Dark fae would be best. I'll go in with Titus on the other side and hopefully one of us can stop him from drawing attention. Carmine will stay here with Ia."

"I will fucking not!" I burst out, the profanity slipping easily from my lips. "I am over this infantilizing shit, Draven. You can't wrap me in cotton."

He rounds on me, bringing our faces so close together, I can see flecks of burnished gold in the center of his eyes, standing out from the darkness. How had I never noticed it before?

His scent is thick in my nose, the warmth of him tantalizingly close. If we were alone, the palpable sense of danger emanating from him would have turned me on.

"I am trying to keep you *alive,* Carmine. It's not time for you to face them. Your skills are underdeveloped. A handful of dark fae and a walking church brought your other half to the surface. You think you won't be consumed by it if you have to face a stronger foe? If you survive at all?"

My body's first, traitorous reaction is to flinch away from the accusation. Tears form in my eyes, willing to fall. I blink them back. How am I ever to prove myself if no one gives me the chance? It hurts all the more that it's Draven saying these things. Draven, who's always supported me, loved me from afar. If he doesn't believe in me, how can I be sure of myself?

"I can make Sabre see sense, Draven. I know I can. And you're wasting time arguing. We have to go now, if we want to salvage the situation and get those stones. So are you going to bitch at me, or are we going to seize the stones?"

I can see the struggle play out on his face, see the stubborn resolve waver as passion battles with duty. I can tell the exact moment his resolution buckles. I smile, faintly. Finally I've gained some sort of ground.

He jabs a finger at me. "You don't go running into trouble. You just drag Sabre out, got it? We'll get the stones."

I give him a mock salute and a more genuine smile.

Draven steps closer, erasing the space between us. His large, rough hands cup either side of my face and then he kisses me. It's a brief, tense liplock and then he releases me, turning on one heel so he can crest the dune as well. And as one, we all begin forward, some of us moving faster than others.

We're fortunate in at least one regard. The sand makes moving slow, so by the time we've slid down the dune and started climbing another, we can still see Sabre, not quite at the edge of the revelry. We may just catch up to him before he can reach the line of centaurs. Maybe isn't good enough for me, though. There has to be something I can do to salvage this situation…

It comes to me in a flash of insight and I crouch, placing my hand on the cooling sand. It's more difficult to dredge up power here, where the land is so arid. The last time I tried this, it was as easy as breathing. The land in Wonderland is so fecund, almost anything can be coaxed from the soil. Not here though. Anything I summon will wither and die in a matter of minutes. But those minutes could be the tipping point between a controlled mission and absolute anarchy.

Buquor, a spiny, highly poisonous desert plant I've only ever read about could possibly grow here. The problem? One prick of the thorns will be deadly to any of my compatriots. But, since I literally carry poison in my skin, I might be immune. It will hurt, but a little pain is worth it to stop the certain death that will follow our discovery. So I concentrate, pull my power to the fore and slam it into the ground, keeping the color illustration fixed firmly in front of my mind.

Moments later, a slab of the stuff, thick as a paving stone, springs up from the sand, seemingly with no roots beneath. It'll wither the second I release it. It's good enough. With more concentration, more Buquor appears, popping up through the sand like mushrooms after rain.

"Don't walk on it," I warn the rest as I climb on the first slab. "It's poisoned."

And then I run, biting my lip to contain cries of agony as the three-inch spines stab through my boots and into the tender arches of my feet. It's not long before a small puddle of blood sloshes about in my boots, making the footing even trickier. I press on, because it's faster than wading through sand.

Sabre has reached the edge of the revelry now, and there's a naked blade in his hand. A shortsword or perhaps his signature saber. I can't tell. He's scanning the crowd with the keen eyes of a predator searching for prey. I don't dare shout his name. I'm close, so I think he might hear me. Then again, the grunts and moans of rutting creatures are just one layer of the discordant sound the revelry makes. He may be deaf to anything but his own heartbeat.

I leap off my improvised pathway and land in the sand with a squelching sound. This close, the reek of spirits singes my nostrils and makes bile scald my throat. I've never liked spirits. I don't like the smell, don't like the taste, and I don't like what it does to men. Now it seems like I'm set to wade into a river of it. Taking in the last semi-pure breath I'm likely to have for a while, I plunge into the crowd.

I'm almost knocked to the ground the second I do. I bump hard into the flank of a centaur, skid in mud, and barely avoid being whipped across the face by its tail. I'm incredibly fortunate to be crouching in an attempt to catch myself, because it's scanning the area to see what's just struck it.

He's got a woman (perhaps a maenad?) speared on a cock that's truly massive. She wriggles in his arms, face contorted in an expression that could be pleasure or pain. I don't have long to examine it because I'm off, trying to keep sight of Sabre's retreating back.

It's almost a dance, trying to avoid the stomping hooves, the women being pushed this way and that, their backsides in the air, their heads thrown back in ecstasy. Sex fugs the air, thick and pungent here, the chorus of moans almost drowning out the thrumming beat of the drums and stringed instruments coming from further into the circle.

It's so tempting to give into the pull of the music. Sway a little, perhaps try the wine. Just a sip… It would be incredible to be bent over and fucked properly, wouldn't it? I could just…

I catch myself at last, just before I can approach a centaur. Draven might forgive me dalliances with his brothers, but I don't think he could stand to see me being fucked violently by a malevolent enemy centaur.

Right... bad idea.

I trudge through the muck as best I can and finally tug Sabre to a stop. He whirls, blade flashing up from the line of his leg into a ready position as he turns on me. Reason doesn't enter his eyes immediately, and there's a terrifying second where I think he'll stab me.

Then the point drops away from my throat and something like guilt seeps into those cold blue eyes.

"Carmine? What are you doing here?"

"Trying to stop you," I hiss, counting on my voice to be drowned by the roar of the crowd. "We can't be seen here, Sabre. If you kill Arcadius, you're going to end up getting the rest of us slaughtered."

He drops his gaze to the ground and takes a deep breath. When he lifts his eyes to mine again, they're sober. "I... I wasn't thinking." His gaze flicks longingly toward a point just off to our right. "He's just... so close, Carmine. I could..."

"Slay him in front of all of his friends? Yes, that will end well. Why don't you just instigate a stampede? That will at least ensure the rest of us die more quickly."

"I can't let Arcadius live, Carmine." He insists. "Not after what he did to my mother."

I stay very still for a few seconds, trying to formulate a plan. It's not a good idea.

But, I'm not able to get far with my less than great idea because I'm suddenly seized by my hair from behind. I turn to look and see a horse's knobby knees pressing into my back.

"Too many clothes, girl," a man's voice says on a nicker. I don't have to crane my neck to guess what's behind me. "Strip and let a real man take you."

"I've got one," I snap, stepping into Sabre. With his hair half-loose from its usual tail and half-splattered with filth, he looks almost like one of the dark fae nearer the center.

A glance backwards confirms my suspicions. It's a massive brute, with the coat and markings of a dapple gray, the bulging muscle of a male in his prime, and thick blonde hair that tumbles around his shoulders. He glares down at us suspiciously. I try to keep my head tucked down. I don't know how many of these monsters will know me by sight, but it's insane to risk it.

"Prove it then," the centaur orders and then looks to Sabre before returning his gaze to me. "Fuck him, girl. What else are you here for?"

Sabre opens his mouth, begins to protest, but doesn't get a word out before I push myself at him. I smack hard against his chest and almost wince. Good Gods, are they all built of bricks rather than muscle? I've never met another body with less yield than my hunstmen.

Sabre's arms lock around me almost at once, bracketing my waist, holding us so we touch from the chest down. We're so close, I can feel the ragged beat of his heart, hear the labored breaths he drags in.

"Carmine…" he whispers, the sound too low to be heard over the crowd. "We can't. I won't impugn your honor in such a fashion."

"I'm not worried about my virtue, Sabre," I murmur, tracing the shell of his ear with my lips. I nip the lobe and he actually draws in a sharp breath. "Are you worried about yours?"

"No."

"Then what are you waiting for?"

"Draven," he starts.

"Will understand," I answer and then look up at the centaur who still stares down at me. I turn back to Sabre. "Draven would much rather it be you inside me than him."

Sabre nods, almost to himself. He lets me step back and I begin stripping off my layers the moment I have confirmation from him, dropping them to the ground. They're almost immediately swallowed by the mud. I think I toss the coat far enough away for it to be salvageable, but the remnants of my shirt, which I'd been using to bind my breasts, are lost immediately in the mire. The trousers are trampled in the next few seconds. It really doesn't matter so long as I can salvage the coat, with its many roomy, magicked pockets. There are weapons I can use in some, and plenty of space to store the stones as well.

My smallclothes come off last, fluttering to the muddy ground like a thin strip of paper, immediately lost to the filth. Eyes fix on me from all sides, and I fight not to let the embarrassment show on my face when lewd comments are tossed my way. Several centaurs elucidate in excruciating detail what they'd love to do to my ass. I ignore them, seeking out the only pair of eyes that truly matter in this chaos.

Sabre's gaze is fastened on me and his tongue flicks out to lick his bottom lip in an almost anxious fashion. He still makes no move to do more. I suppose I'll have to be the instigator then. I leap at him, wanting him to take me to the ground. He lets out a soft sound of surprise as we topple toward the ground. Mud splatters in every direction, and allows us a little room as the centaurs circle to avoid it hitting their magnificent tails or the partners they're currently inside. The white brilliance of Sabre's hair is lost in the muck, but it doesn't seem to upset him.

His eyes grow a little round when I clamber on top of him, hugging his hips between my thighs. Hunger flickers in his gaze when I trace a hand down my body, drawing his eyes across all the things he could be touching if he weren't so intent on being a gentleman. An actual moan tears its way from his throat when I find my clit and begin stroking slow circles over it, rolling my hips over his.

"Fuck, Carmine..."

"That's the idea," I say with a small smirk. "Are you going to get to it, or shall I?"

Sabre reaches for his belt at last, struggling with the latch even as our audience laughs. For the first time, I'm incredibly grateful this place stinks and is filthy. They can barely see us, can barely hear us, and we're only two bodies in the crowd. I never imagined having an audience for this, but if it keeps us alive...

And I can't deny I've wanted to experience Sabre from the first time I saw him. Would I have pined for them equally if I'd met them all at the same time? I think so. Neva's brief conversations with me had been illuminating. I'd always believed the tales of two people being destined for one another. I'd always thought it would be Draven and me. But now I know the heart can grow, can accept more people than the limited number I've assigned mine. I could love Draven *and* his brothers.

In fact, I already do.

Sabre finally gets the belt free and unfastens his buttons, shoving the trousers down the second he can. His manhood springs free and... Gods, how are they all so large? I'm afraid it will split me in two. Not as intimidating as a centaur's cock, perhaps, but close. Still, I don't let it deter me for long. Shimmying back up his hips, I poise just above him, letting his head slide between my folds teasingly before easing the tip of him inside.

He lets out a swear word so loud, it draws more snickers from the centaurs around us. I ease myself, inch by inch, down his shaft, moaning a little as he fills me completely. I shudder and still when he's completely inside. I can't help but shift a few inches to ease the feeling that I might simply combust. He's so *big*...

Sabre seizes my hips with a savage growl that raises goosebumps all along my body. My nipples harden to painful points. His nails dig furrows into my hips as he thrusts himself up harder, rolls my hips so I drag along the length of him. I keen, arch my back, and cry out.

He guides me so I'm riding him hard and fast, not releasing me until he's sure I have the rhythm. And when he is sure, his nimble fingers slide up my stomach to cup my breasts. He plucks at the nipples hard enough I choke on a sob of pleasure. They're still tender from Titus' recent ministrations.

I'm patterned with bruises and bites and I can't seem to care about any of them. I just want this

feeling to keep going, unending, forever in this
moment with Sabre. Bliss washes over us, and I'm
certain the magic of the revelry takes us over for a
time.

All I can feel is the harness of him in me,
warmth everywhere he touches me, the bliss of
having my mind sponged away so all I care about
is the music, the bodies around me, the one under
me, and the wonder of not thinking.

Even the air smells wonderful, the reek of
spirits somehow transforming into a spicy perfume.
The fug of sex, spirits, and magic in the air is so
intoxicating, I could sing, perhaps dance. I barely
register when Sabre pulls out of me, except to
mourn the loss of his hard length for a moment.
Then he's guiding me onto my knees, seizing a
handful of my hair and pulling, even as he sheathes
himself inside me again.

He's so forceful. I want this, want him. I never
want to let go...

I'm chorusing words I don't know, in some
primeval tongue that far predates me. May predate
the stars. But it only drives the frenzy up higher
and higher, until even the points of light in the
night sky seem to cavort in dizzying jigs. Illusion,
or coming madness, I can't tell.

The spell is broken when Sabre stills behind
me, hips jerking one final time as he spills his seed.

I can feel it all over my thighs. Has he spilled several times? Have I been that unaware?

I can tell reason has returned to him because he draws out of me slowly, with more care than he's taken with me this entire time. Eventually, I want him to take me, no holds barred, but this isn't the night for it.

He leans over my back and to the others it might appear he's whispering more filth into my ear. His breath tickles the nape of my neck when he places a gentle kiss in the hollow just beneath my ear.

"Are you alright?"

"Fine," I murmur. Then louder; "Let's find a place a little less crowded, lover."

I squirm out from beneath him and turn, knees squelching in the mud. Sabre flashes me an almost wicked grin for a few seconds, and then it evaporates when we both recall where we are and what we're here to do.

He slides his hand into mine and tugs me up. He hikes the trousers up just enough to cover his cock but doesn't bother to button them. I stoop to retrieve my coat and use it in a lackluster attempt to cover myself, eliciting more interest from the crowd.

We've nearly made it to the outskirts of the circle now. I think I can guess Sabre's plans well enough. Edge around the base of the mountain and take out whatever guards might be waiting, fucking ourselves silly along the way if need be.

But that plan is thoroughly scuppered when a large pair of hooves impacts the ground just ahead, sending mud and dark wine sloshing in every direction. I follow the line of the creature's body up and up, swallowing hard when I see the enormous, dark-skinned centaur with a broadsword.

"Halt," he rumbles. "Who are you?"

Sabre's lips are pale and pressed into a tight line of rage. I know precisely what he's going to do the second before he does it. Because there's no one else this man can be.

"Your end, Arcadius," Sabre growls.

Then he plucks the feather from the end of his sullied, half-done braid and breaks the tip off before he plunges it deep into the centaur's gut. Almost at once, skin begins to balloon as gas fills Arcadius' abdomen. Black lesions spiral out from the wound site and the centaur's legs buckle slowly. The broadsword topples to the ground, and I heave the heavy thing into my arms. I have a feeling I'll need it soon.

Arcadius' body falls sideways, almost crushing another centaur flat. Heads turn and finally locate us standing over the felled monster. All goes still and silent for a terrifying half-second. Then the howls, the yells, the caterwauls begin. The drums begin again, this time deep, booming war drums.

We've been outed.
Fuck.

TWENTY-TWO
DRAVEN

A pile of glittering stones lies at the base of the huge bonfire. They're mundane rock at the moment, though I can see a few beginning to glow as we approach. Neva's camouflage is incredible, but blood will out. Those stones sense a fraction of Morningstar's power nearby. I can only hope the orange glow of the fire will disguise the stones' response.

We appear to be a group of dark fae and a centaur approaching the inner circle. We're conspicuous enough on our own. The centaurs seem to keep to the outer circle, fucking with wild abandon while the inner circles seem to be more involved in chanting. I think this hedonistic revelry has to be leading up to something. There's a sort of tension in the air, like the crackle of ozone just before the storm hits. Something is very, very wrong...

"They're casting," Neva murmurs, stepping over the wriggling form of a maenad who barely seems to notice her. They're all so consumed with what they're doing.

"Yes," Hattie agrees. "They're working on… something large."

"Any idea what?" I ask.

Hattie and Neva exchange a glance then finally shake their heads.

"No," Neva says. "But odds are, it's not good."

I don't say anything to that, feeling a cutting remark about the uselessness of witches wouldn't help our cause at the moment. We're finally at the edge, and Hattie seizes me by the hand with another of those manic grins, spinning me like a top before looping her arm into mine.

"What the hell are you doing?"

"*We* are dancing. Don't you want to get close enough to snatch the stones?"

Of course I do, but making myself sick in the process wasn't part of our plan. Still, I let the Mad Madam pull me into a reel. We dance closer and closer, until my head is spinning and the heat of the fire seems to sink through my skin and down into my bones. The damn thing is so hot, one could probably fry an egg on the ground near it. Every instinct tells me to get as far away as I can.

Then, with a suddenness that startles me, Hattie releases me. I windmill my arms, try to catch myself before I can fall, but it's no use. I land on my ass… right on the pile of stones.

Ah, there was the method to the fucking madness. Now I just look like a clumsy oaf, instead of a thief. I grab a handful of the stones, shoving them into one of the seemingly endless pockets the coat has to offer. Then I stuff in another. Three is all I think I can manage without giving the game away.

I stand, brushing myself off and bow toward the figure reclining on the chair near the fire.

Deianira is quite beautiful. I'm sure she has men and women who worship her as the pinnacle of perfection. But I've seen Carmine bare and laid out on the grass before me, so I know what true perfection looks like.

Still, her milky skin is unblemished and glows in the light of the fire, so she's painted in golden light. Her legs are long and lean, the juncture of her legs bare and glistening. She rubs small circles into her pearl, smiling idly at her lover. She flicks a glance to me after just a moment. Her dark curls tumble artfully around her shoulders and her dark eyes smolder in the low light.

"Go. Find your master, you fool. Tell Septimus we'll have no need of his roaches soon. The seal is beginning to crumble. Can't you feel it?"

I still, ice sloshing through my veins, the horror of those two sentences freezing me in place.

The seals are breaking.

They're not fucking, fighting, and bloodletting at the base of this mountain for the pleasure of it. They're trying to break down the last of the seals.

If Septimus gets out, that means the rest should be coming as well. They're going to release the other six.

I open my mouth to scream at Neva. Surely, with her newly found powers, she could find a way to slaughter every single reveler in one go. Stop the ritual in its tracks. But by the time I can find the breath to form the words, it's too late.

There's a colossal boom, like the gates of Avernus themselves have been knocked off their hinges and brilliant lights and colors shoot over the mountain, streaking like comets into the far distance.

Green for Vita, a red-orange for Sol, a silver-gray for Lycaon, crimson for Hassan, white-gold for Bacchus and finally, an oozing black ribbon that's so dark, it blots out the stars as it travels along its path.

"Gods," I breathe, too horrified to do anything but stare at the point where they disappeared. "The crazy fuckers did it. They released them. Morningstar's out."

Then, at some signal that I seem to have missed, the crowd falls silent. A good half-second passes, and at first I think it's a moment of respectful silence for their liberated comrades. But, I'm wrong.

"Intruders!" Deianira shrieks. "Find them! Kill them!"

Chaos erupts in the camp and there's only one thing to do now.

"Run!"

TWENTY-THREE
CARMINE

Sabre slashes our way free of the first row of legs, arms, and wings, toppling several centaurs as we go.

It's not enough.

They swarm us like angry bees, and from every side there are new elbows, knees, hands, and more to batter us. Every part of me hurts, and not even in the deliciously pleasant way my men can illicit. Every second threatens to bring us down to our knees and from there, to be trampled underfoot.

Only Sabre's hand in mine keeps me upright. He drags us forward, seeming to keep on his feet out of sheer contrariness.

"I'm sorry, Carmine," he pants. "I'm so sorry. I shouldn't have…"

"Just get us out of here."

All the apologies in the world don't change the fact we've been caught. If by some miracle we wrestle our way free, I fear we'll be the only ones who survive this night. The others must be deeper inside, trying to locate the stones. So close to the goddess and her lover? I doubt they'll survive.

The thought makes my breath catch and fresh agony ripples through me. Titus and Draven, gone? Neva, trampled to death, her beautiful face only so much bloody meat on the ground? No! No! I can't lose any of them. Not when I've only just gotten used to having them in my life.

Up ahead, there's a break in the crowd and beyond that, the white desert sands. I'm alarmed to see the moon is sinking lower in the sky, hovering just above the line of dunes. How long were Sabre and I lost in the revelry's magic, fucking each other senseless?

We burst from the crowd like spurts of blood from a jagged wound. Sabre sweeps his sword into guard position, finally releasing me now that I'm not in danger of being trampled. Then he stops dead, skidding to a halt in the mud.

Now, I see why the crowd parted. It's not a break in the line after all, but a pocket to trap us on all sides. There are centaurs and satyrs at our backs and a lone female figure blocking our egress just ahead.

She's incredibly beautiful, putting even the maenads to shame. She seems to have swallowed moonlight, and the luminescence shines through her skin. Her hair is wild disarray, like it's been fisted in the hand of a man while he rutted her. Every inch of her is flawless ivory, except for her lips and cheeks, which seem to have been rouged with blood.

It's like looking at a mirror image of Neva, cracked and distorted. Beautiful but wrong. The resemblance is passing and when I blink, I can spy still more wrong with the picture. Her eyes are dark, pitiless pools of black, the teeth behind her lips needle-sharp, like a blood drinker's. Those night-dark eyes flick between us, running contemptuously over me in particular.

"So this mewling little kitten is meant to unseat my father?" She laughs. "I couldn't believe it when Thilde reported back to me, but it must be true."

I feel about three inches tall as she stares me down. Power fairly radiates off her. How in the name of Avernus am I meant to defeat something like her, let alone her father, who is no doubt worse?

I draw myself up to my full height. No matter how frightened I am, a refuse to cower. I won't mewl or cry, the way she clearly expects. If I'm to die here, I'll do it putting up a fight. I'll do it honoring the memory of my mother and father, who had both tried to protect me in their own ways.

"Watch who you're calling kitten," I snap. The crowd has quitted to a dull roar, so my words can be heard above the general din.

I step forward and Sabre automatically tries to cover me, tries to put his body between me and the goddess, hate blazing in her eyes. I nudge him aside, shaking my head.

"This is my fight, Sabre. Find the others. Get them out of here."

"I'm not leaving your side!"

"Fine. Shield yourself then. This is going to get ugly."

There's not much time for him to respond.

I draw inward, prodding at the beast that lays beneath my skin. It's been cudgeled into submission by my mother and uncle most of my life. Now all it wants is blood and terror. The ground runs red with blood, which is a good start, and now it wants a feast of fear. This time, I don't let it overwhelm me, I just ride the tide as it comes.

Claws sprout from my nail beds, hissing and spitting sparks when I run them along the edge of the heavy broadsword. My strength rises with the hag's emergence, and I'm able to heft it onto one shoulder. My eyes itch, and I'm told they fill entirely with silver that will eventually bleed onto the rest of my face.

Cold fear rides the breeze coming off Mount Vallis and stirs every person in the crowd. Nervous knickers go up from the centaurs, bleats from the satyrs, and small shrieks from the maenads.

Instinctually, I reach down toward the ground, dredging up what the soil will allow. Vines spring into my hands, already budding with flowers. They wind up my arms, over my shoulders and then lash around my torso, covering me as thoroughly as any chain mail. I don't stop calling for them, feeding more and more into my hands until I'm fully girded in verdant armor, and a strand as thick as a bullwhip heaves my sword aloft. It reminds me of Titus' chain scythe, though far more unwieldy.

More and more, I draw life from the silty ground, and flowers and vines sprout with incredible speed. Aconite, hemlock, nightshade all bloom and perfume the air. Drecaine vines wind upward and knot together above our heads, forming a deadly cage around us. There's perhaps six feet total between the goddess and me. Anyone who tries to approach will die a very lingering death.

Unfortunately, Sabre might as well, if I'm unlucky. He's trapped in the cage as well and I don't have time to release him. Deianira may use the opportunity to escape. I'll have to trust he's capable.

Deianira's lips part to reveal those needle fangs. "Ah, that's more like it. Let's see what you can do, little hag."

"That's Princess Carmine to you, bitch," I huff, flexing my control over the vines holding the broadsword.

Beside me, Sabre shifts into a ready position as well. Feet apart, saber at the ready, his chin held

high. Something in his face has relaxed and it
makes him somehow more attractive. I hadn't
realized there's been tension in his body since that
day in the cabin, when we discovered we'd be
facing Bacchus' revelry. Perhaps now that he's
slain his mother's killer, he can have some measure
of peace. I'd like to know what he's like without
that weighing heavy on his shoulders.

I don't see Deianira move. One moment she's
standing six feet away from me, the next she's so
near, I can smell the wine she's been drinking. It
saturates her skin. Too close to swing the sword
and too awkward an angle to allow for a thrust into
her back. The sword is huge, built for a creature
much larger than I, and would probably skewer me
as well.

Her fist slams into my breastbone with enough
force to drive the air from my lungs. Agony lances
through my chest and I swear I feel bone grind
beneath her knuckles.

My back hits the net of Drecaine vines, and
they're supple enough that I'm able to take the
impact with minimal injury. I twine my fingers
around the nearest and, imitating a move I've seen
Draven execute, swing my legs upward, using the
heel of one bare foot to bat her head to the side.

If I'd been wearing a boot, I might have been
able to break her jaw. As it is, she rocks backward,
baring her needle teeth again. She produces a blade

(I'm not sure from where, since she's not wearing a stitch of clothing) and comes after me again. A trail of silver fire follows her blade. I duck the blow in time to avoid having my throat slashed, but the fire follows in the wake of the blade, striking at me like a bullwhip. The spell finds its mark, wrapping around my throat and pulling taught like a noose.

The spellwork begins to burn almost at once, eating away at the vine armor I've made for myself, trailing agonizing heat down my front. She'll burn me alive. Or maybe the fiery noose will end me first. Already black spots are bursting like leaden bubbles in front of my eyes.

Then Sabre's sword flashes down, cutting through the flaming spell like it's made of tissue. The pressure finally lets up and I'm able to gasp in a breath. Through streaming eyes, I see him advance on Deianira, sword raised. My heart hammers against my ribs and I want to shout at him to squirm through the bars and run. I can't watch him die on my behalf. Even if he does manage to end Deianira, there's still a host of creatures that will come after us. We could simply be trampled underfoot by accident.

And then an enormous shape looms over us, blotting out most of the orangey glow of the fire. I crane my neck, though the very action feels like it should separate my head from my shoulders. I'll likely have a brand there for life.

An enormous black shape has hooked a claw into the top of the vine cage and is dragging it up and off us. I snatch one of the vines almost on reflex and clasp it as tightly as I can. Almost at once, the giant raven form of Draven begins to lift me from the ground. There's a problem though. Sabre can't grab hold. Not without poisoning himself. I crane my neck desperately. We'll be too far off the ground to do much soon. None of the others circling above can swoop in to save him, lest they be skewered by swords, spears, and arrows. But if nothing's done, he'll die anyway.

"My leg!" I shout at him. "Grab my leg."

Sabre hesitates only a fraction of a second before doing what I ordered. His grip is almost crushing on my calf, but I bite back the cry that builds in my throat. I still don't scream when we're hauled upward and the motion almost wrenches my hip from its socket. Deianira does enough screaming for me, shrieking wordless fury at the sky as we rise up and up. By the time any of them have knocked arrows, it's too late. We're far out of range, rising to a point in the sky where the air drops frigid water onto my arms and face.

I'm in too much pain to ask the burning questions. Was this all a waste? Did we come here, risk so much, and accomplish nothing?

The link is wavering between us, but Draven is able to send one last thought to me before Hattie's magic breaks utterly.

"We have the stones, Carmine. Don't worry. I have you. You're safe now."

And through the pain, I smile.

At fucking last.

Something has gone right.

EPILOGUE
CARMINE

The next weeks are a hectic blur of happenings.

Draven and the others insisted on making a detour to the House of Corvid before we made our way back to Ascor. The accommodations were pleasant, with a barracks that was a little spartan but still comfortable. To my amusement, a schedule was arranged on who was sleeping with whom. The beds were too narrow to allow for more than two at a time, and every single man wanted to sleep with his woman. Neva and I stood by, arms crossed as the men argued over who would share our beds on any given night.

Of particular curiosity was the glass case set up in the main hall. Within was a man. Handsome, by anyone's estimation, with dark hair, a striking face, and a lean, fit body to accompany it. He looks as though he could wake at any moment. They told me he was the Prince of Delorood, Andric, and that he's frozen in a death sleep, unable to be woken without the proper catalyst. I wish I could rouse him. But I have my own problems to worry about.

Even with the ambrosia forced into me and Ia's care, the damage from Deianira's flame spell was permanent. I have a circular scar just beneath my chin where the skin blackened and shriveled. I'll likely carry this scar with me to the grave. None of my men can keep their fingers from straying to it from time to time.

Uncle Spryros' conspiracy was unveiled to the people when we returned to Ascor. By a fortunate turn of events, all three huntsmen's signet rings lit up when we strode into the throne room after a very brief siege by a dragon. None of Uncle's advisors said a word when the huntsmen struck him down. I thought Titus and Draven might have been a little too gleeful to carry out his execution. At least Sabre stopped them from making a mess of it. Efficient in all things, my Sabre.

The coronation came quickly after, done without much pomp. Necessary, now that the seals have completely eroded. Morningstar and the others are out, their scheme to gather worshippers revealed, and their followers outed. Most of Fantasia is preparing for war. Whose side the others will join is anyone's guess. But Ascor stands with Delorood. I can only hope more will claim the same.

I hadn't expected my speeches to rally the people. I've always been fairly innocuous. A wilting flower hidden in a shady corner. It's so strange to be a figurehead, always in the thick of things.

The stones are being sent out. As much as I hate parting with them, I've decided we need to distribute them to other Guild factions throughout Fantasia. Draven will be staying as my loyal bodyguard, as he has for many years. Though now he also has privileges as my consort. They all do.

Soon we'll be able to scout for Chosen Ones on our own, instead of happening on them by chance. Perhaps we can train them before the real fight begins in order to prevent disastrous confrontations like the ones Neva and I have found ourselves in.

Titus is currently on his way to contact one of the only dark fae that have joined our side. Her dragon lover, Veles, is apparently the father of Malvolo, Herrick, and Reve. Four of his children were killed in the last war. He wants vengeance. Their charge, Briar, is suspected to be Chosen. I sincerely hope so.

With Briar, that will bring our total up to five.

Five of ten.

It puts us that much closer.

Halfway there.

Half of a nation's hope.

Halfway to freedom.

Watch out Morningstar.

Ready or not, here we come.

To Be Continued in:

BRIAR
NOW AVAILABLE!

Get FREE E-Books!
It's as easy as:

1. Go to my website: www.hpmallory.com
2. Sign up in the pop-up box or on the link at the top of the home page
3. Check your email!

HP MALLORY is a New York Times and USA Today Bestselling Author!

She lives in Southern California with her son, where she is at work on her next book.

Printed in Great Britain
by Amazon

82801875R00169